THE
TESTAMENTS

Margaret Atwood

*sparknotes

© 2020 SparkNotes LLC

This 2020 edition printed for SparkNotes LLC by Sterling Publishing Co.

ISBN 978-1-4114-8042-1

Distributed in Canada by Sterling Publishing Co., Inc.
c/o Canadian Manda Group, 664 Annette Street
Toronto, Ontario M6S 2C8, Canada
Distributed in the United Kingdom by GMC Distribution Services
Castle Place, 166 High Street, Lewes, East Sussex BN7 1XU, England
Distributed in Australia by NewSouth Books
University of New South Wales, Sydney, NSW 2052, Australia

For information about custom editions, special sales, and premium
and corporate purchases, please contact Sterling Special Sales at
800-805-5489 or specialsales@sterlingpublishing.com.

Manufactured in Canada

Lot #:
2 4 6 8 10 9 7 5 3 1
09/20

sterlingpublishing.com
sparknotes.com

Please email content@sparknotes.com to report any errors.

CONTENTS

CONTEXT

Margaret Atwood is one of Canada's most decorated and beloved authors. Although she has published several books of poetry and critical essays, Atwood remains best known for her many novels, two of which have received one of fiction's most prestigious honors: the Booker Prize. Atwood was born in 1939 in Ottawa, Ontario, Canada, and she spent much of her childhood in the heavily forested areas of northern Quebec. An insatiable reader from childhood on, Atwood felt inclined to a writing career from an early age. She pursued literary studies at the University of Toronto, where she received a bachelor's degree in 1961, and then at Harvard University, where she completed a master's degree in 1962. Atwood began work on a doctoral degree, but her dissertation, which she never finished, took a back seat as her writing career took off. She published her first book of poetry, *Double Persephone*, in 1961. Her first novel, *The Edible Woman*, appeared eight years later. Atwood has since published a number of significant novels, including *The Handmaid's Tale* (1985), *Cat's Eye* (1988), *Alias Grace* (1996), *The Blind Assassin* (2000), *The Testaments* (2019), and a trio of dystopian novels known collectively as the MaddAddam Trilogy (2003–2013).

Throughout her long and prolific career, Atwood has made a name for herself by depicting a diverse range of female characters, often portraying their struggles to survive the harsh and constricting conditions of a patriarchal society. In her first novel, *The Edible Woman*, Atwood's protagonist Marian comes to suspect that men have little real respect for her and would simply prefer to "consume" her before moving on to the next woman. Atwood takes her critique of patriarchal attitudes further in *The Handmaid's Tale*, which offers a vision of a dystopian future in which women have lost nearly all of their agency to authoritarian male leaders. Many of Atwood's subsequent novels continue to explore the lives of different types of women. In *Alias Grace,* Atwood provides a fictionalized account of the notorious nineteenth-century Canadian "murderess" Grace Marks. *The Blind Assassin* weaves a mystery out of the lives of two sisters. Finally, *The Penelopiad* (2005) offers a feminist revision of Greek mythology told from the perspective of

Odysseus's wife, Penelope, who looks back on her life from the land of the dead.

The publication in 1985 of *The Handmaid's Tale* marked the beginning of Atwood's interest in speculative fiction, a broad category of fiction that imagines what could become of the world given the current social, political, and technological state of affairs. Although some critics believe that science fiction and fantasy belong under the umbrella of speculative fiction, Atwood distances herself from these genres. As she has stated in numerous public interviews, she understands science fiction as a genre that imagines a world filled with futuristic technologies that do not yet exist. By contrast, speculative fiction imagines events that could really happen given the political and technological means that are already part of our world. In the case of *The Handmaid's Tale*, for example, Atwood explored the possibility of a near future in which a totalitarian state replaces the United States government and institutes the Republic of Gilead, a repressive patriarchal regime that strips women of their rights. The dystopian world Atwood imagines in *The Handmaid's Tale* could potentially come to be, and this plausibility gives the novel both its power and relevance for contemporary readers.

In recent years, *The Handmaid's Tale* achieved a new relevance which inspired a sequel: *The Testaments*. The resurgence of interest in *The Handmaid's Tale* relates closely to the release of Hulu's adaptation of the novel for television. The first three seasons of the show earned popular and critical acclaim, and they have drawn a new generation of readers to Atwood's work. As a response to the surge of renewed interest in *The Handmaid's Tale*, Atwood decided to write a sequel to her landmark novel. *The Testaments*, which appeared in September 2019, returns readers to the dystopian world of Gilead approximately fifteen years after the events depicted in *The Handmaid's Tale*. Instead of focusing on the fate of Offred, the protagonist from the earlier novel, the sequel follows three very different women whose lives converge at a crucial moment to exploit the weakness in Gilead's oppressive theocratic regime. Like its predecessor, *The Testaments* has received widespread popular and critical praise. The novel also earned Atwood the second Booker Prize of her remarkable career.

PLOT OVERVIEW

T

he Testaments braids together three separate first-person testimonies, each of which corresponds to one of the novel's three narrators. The first narrator, Aunt Lydia, composes her account in a manuscript known as "The Ardua Hall Holograph." The other two narrators, Agnes and Daisy, each give spoken accounts, which appear in the novel as transcripts of witness testimonies. Each of the three narrators tells the story of her role in a conspiracy to topple the patriarchal and theocratic regime of the Republic of Gilead.

In "The Ardua Hall Holograph," Aunt Lydia charts her rise to power within Gilead. Prior to the coup that brought down the United States government, Aunt Lydia had had an accomplished career as a judge. She tells of her arrest and her experience of being held in a stadium, where she watched as members of the new regime executed other professional women. As the days passed, Aunt Lydia saw that women were replacing men as the executioners.

One night, men came for Aunt Lydia and escorted her to a man named Commander Judd. He asked her if she would cooperate with the regime. When she hesitated, he dispatched her to several days of solitary confinement, after which she agreed to cooperate. Despite knowing that she would have to participate in the execution of other women, Aunt Lydia decided to do whatever was necessary to survive and take Gilead down from within. Alongside three other women—Elizabeth, Helena, and Vidala—she became one of the Founders of the Aunts. The Founders were responsible for drafting and enforcing the laws that governed all women in Gilead. Aunt Lydia quickly gained dominance over the other Founders and sought ways to play the three against each other. In the time since Gilead's founding, Aunt Lydia has established a vast network of surveillance equipment to collect evidence of others' indiscretions.

As Aunt Lydia composes her manuscript, she is actively engaged in tracking the whereabouts of "Baby Nicole," a child famously smuggled out of Gilead and into Canada many years earlier by her Handmaid mother. Baby Nicole's whereabouts remain concealed by operatives of an anti-Gilead resistance group called Mayday.

The novel's other two narratives feature two young women: one who grew up in Gilead, and one who grew up in Canada. These

3

PLOT OVERVIEW

women become involved in a plot spearheaded by Aunt Lydia to topple Gilead.

Agnes Jemima grew up in a privileged Gilead family. Her happy childhood ended abruptly when her mother, Tabitha, died and her emotionally remote father married a cruel widow named Paula. Agnes had been anxious about Gilead's treatment of women from an early age. Her fears were confirmed when she witnessed the horrific death in childbirth of her family's Handmaid. When Agnes reached the age of thirteen, Paula sought to marry her off to Commander Judd. One of Agnes's school friends, Becka, attempted suicide to escape her own marriage, and Agnes contemplated a similar course. But one day, Aunt Lydia paid her a visit and suggested that she avoid marriage by taking refuge among the Aunts.

Agnes found a way to maneuver around Paula and successfully pledge as a Supplicant. Once she arrived safely at Ardua Hall, Agnes was reunited with Becka, who had also pledged. As part of her training, Agnes learned to read and write, two activities forbidden to all women except for Aunts. During this period, she learned that much of Gilead's official theology contradicted the Bible. She also received folders containing top-secret information about corruption among Gilead's elite from an anonymous source. Agnes realized that the Aunts got their power from these secrets, and she hungered for more access to that power.

The third narrator, Daisy, grew up in Toronto, Canada. Her parents, Melanie and Neil, owned and operated a used-clothing store. One day, against her parents' wishes, Daisy attended a protest against human-rights violations in Gilead. When the protest turned violent, she escaped with the help of Ada, a mysterious middle-aged woman who was friends with her mother. That night, Daisy's image appeared on the TV news, scaring her parents.

Not long after, on Daisy's sixteenth birthday, her parents were killed in a car bombing outside their store. Ada picked Daisy up from school and broke the news. With help from some colleagues, Ada set Daisy up in a safehouse on the edge of town. Ada and her colleagues explained that Melanie and Neil weren't Daisy's real parents. Instead, they were Mayday operatives selected to look after her while her real mother remained in hiding. Ada also explained that Daisy was the famous "Baby Nicole" and had been smuggled out of Gilead by her mother, a runaway Handmaid.

Ada and her colleagues explained their commitment to undermine Gilead and how they had a source inside the regime who wanted to send top-secret documents that would help topple the government. However, the deaths of Melanie and Neil had closed their channel of communication with the source, and their only backup plan was to send Daisy into Gilead to retrieve the documents herself. Daisy sneaked into Gilead by pretending to let two missionaries, known as Pearl Girls, convert her.

The three women's lives converged when Daisy arrived at Ardua Hall and Aunt Lydia placed her in Agnes's apartment. In due time, Aunt Lydia revealed herself to Daisy as the source and implanted a minuscule document called a "microdot" containing vast amounts of information about corruption in Gilead into Daisy's arm. She also revealed to Agnes and Daisy that they were sisters. Claiming that she wanted to reform the spiritually rotten core of Gilead, Aunt Lydia enlisted both young women, along with Becka, in a plot to help Daisy escape with her top-secret document cache. Despite a series of complications, Agnes and Daisy successfully escaped to Canada. The incendiary documents immediately hit Canadian media and set the fall of Gilead in motion.

The novel's final section, which takes place far in the future in the year 2197, features a historian named Professor Pieixoto speaking about the written and spoken testimonies that constitute the rest of the book.

CHARACTER LIST

Aunt Lydia A founder of the Gilead order of Aunts. Prior to the coup that overthrew the United States government and established the Republic of Gilead, Aunt Lydia had enjoyed a successful career as a judge. After the transition of power, Aunt Lydia became one of four elite women charged with founding the Aunts, an autonomous order that presided over the laws and regulations governing the lives of Gilead women. She records the story of her conspiracy to topple Gilead in a manuscript later known as "The Ardua Hall Holograph."

Agnes Jemima A young woman from Gilead and an accessory in the plot to bring it down. Agnes grew up in the prominent household of Commander Kyle, where she enjoyed her childhood in the loving care of her adoptive mother, Tabitha. Though always harboring secret doubts about the official laws and theology of Gilead, Agnes showed no signs of outright resistance until her mother's mysterious death and her father's swift remarriage. Flouting her betrothal to the high-ranking Commander Judd, she pledged as a Supplicant in the order of the Aunts. Now known as Aunt Victoria, she desperately wants to learn the truth about her biological mother. Agnes tells her own story in the narrative identified as "Transcript of Witness Testimony 369A."

Daisy A young Canadian woman who learns she was born in Gilead. Daisy grows up believing she's an ordinary Canadian girl, but when her parents, Neil and Melanie, are suddenly murdered with a car bomb, Daisy gets swept into a network of "Mayday" operatives working to take down the Republic of Gilead. The operatives inform her that Neil and Melanie weren't really her parents and that she is actually "Baby Nicole," a child who attained iconic status after getting smuggled out of Gilead. Daisy takes the fake name of Jade and infiltrates Gilead in the hopes of contributing to its collapse. Daisy tells her own story in the narrative identified as "Transcript of Witness Testimony 369B."

Becka   Agnes's classmate, best friend, and fellow Supplicant. Although her father is a dentist and not a Commander, Becka attends a school for elite young girls. She is naturally shy but kind and sensitive. A strong aversion to men leads her to attempt suicide to avoid marriage. She survives and pledges as a Supplicant in the order of the Aunts, in which she adopts the name Aunt Immortelle and plays a role in Aunt Lydia's plan to take down Gilead.

Commander Judd   A high-ranking official who oversees surveillance in Gilead. Commander Judd assisted in planning the coup that overthrew the United States government, and he has served as a prominent official in Gilead since its founding. In his surveillance work, he collaborates closely with Aunt Lydia, who knows the man's history of killing his wives and marrying younger women.

Aunt Vidala   A founder of the Aunts. Aunt Vidala's commitment to Gilead predated the overthrow of the United States government. She bears the traits of a fundamentalist personality and envies Aunt Lydia's authority. She hungers for power and has a penchant for doling out harsh punishments.

Aunt Elizabeth   A founder of the Aunts. Prior to the establishment of Gilead, Aunt Elizabeth worked as an executive assistant to an influential female senator. Though intelligent and experienced in her own right, she readily submits to Aunt Lydia's assertive personality and is caught in the middle of Aunt Vidala and Aunt Lydia's power struggle.

Aunt Helena A founder of the Aunts. Aunt Helena used to work as a public relations representative for a high-fashion lingerie company. Her vanity and lack of self-certainty make her easy for Aunt Lydia to influence.

Tabitha Agnes's adoptive mother. Tabitha had a close and loving relationship with her adopted daughter. Though her love sustained Agnes throughout her childhood, Tabitha died after a protracted illness.

Commander Kyle Agnes's adoptive father. Commander Kyle remained a remote figure throughout Agnes's childhood. Following the death of his wife Tabitha, he grows even less attached to his adopted daughter and schemes with Paula to marry Agnes off.

Paula Agnes's stepmother. The widow of a high-ranking Commander who died in uncertain circumstances, Paula marries Commander Kyle shortly following Tabitha's death. Spiteful and vindictive, she seeks to rid herself of Agnes by marrying her stepdaughter off as quickly as possible.

Ofkyle Handmaid to Commander Kyle. Ofkyle becomes Commander Kyle's Handmaid after he marries Paula. Ofkyle becomes pregnant and carries the child to term but dies in childbirth. The doctor's choice to save the baby over Ofkyle traumatizes Agnes. Later, when Agnes becomes an Aunt, her research in the Bloodlines Genealogical Archives reveals that Ofkyle's real name was Crystal.

Aunt Gabbana A marriage search consultant. Aunt Gabbana oversees all of the arrangements involved in finding Agnes a suitable husband and preparing her wedding.

Aunt Lise A teacher at Rubies Premarital Preparatory. Aunt Lise instructs Agnes and her classmates in the skills they will need as Wives, including food etiquette and flower arranging.

Vera, Rosa, and Zilla Marthas in Commander Kyle's household. All three Marthas have a supportive relationship with Agnes, whom they treat with kindness and dignity, within the limits of Gileadean society. According to Agnes, Vera had a harsh voice, Rosa wore a perpetual scowl, and Zilla spoke softly.

Shunammite Agnes's classmate. Shunammite has an outspoken and frequently belligerent personality. She has a keen awareness of social class from an early age, and as she grows older, she becomes increasingly brash and cruel in pursuit of an elite marriage. She eventually becomes Commander Judd's latest wife.

Dr. Grove Becka's father and a prominent dentist. Dr. Grove serves as the go-to dentist for many important Commanders and their families. His professional reputation wins him many social advantages, including protection from punishment for regularly sexually abusing young women and girls.

Neil Daisy's adoptive father and a secret Mayday operative. Neil is a staunch atheist and enthusiastic collector of cameras. He manages the accounting for the used-clothing shop he runs with his wife. After Neil gets killed by a car bomb, Daisy learns that he isn't her real father but rather a Mayday operative who swore to protect her from Gilead's authorities and to keep her identity secret.

Melanie Daisy's adoptive mother and a secret Mayday operative. Melanie is a fiercely optimistic woman who manages sales and inventory for the used-clothing shop she runs with her husband. After Melanie gets killed by a car bomb, Daisy learns that she isn't her real mother, but rather a Mayday operative who swore to protect her from Gilead's authorities and to keep her identity secret.

CHARACTER LIST

Ada A Mayday operative. Ada takes responsibility for Daisy's well-being after the murders of Neil and Melanie. She recruits Daisy to take part in a plan to infiltrate Gilead and escape with a cache of sensitive information that could be used to take Gilead down.

Elijah A Mayday operative. Elijah informs Daisy of her true identity.

George A Mayday operative. George disguises himself as a homeless man to assist in monitoring and protecting Daisy's identity.

Garth A young Mayday operative. Garth trains Daisy in self-defense in preparation for her entry into Gilead, and she harbors an unspoken crush on him.

Daisy's mother Unnamed. Daisy's mother, who also turns out to be Agnes's mother, appears briefly at the end of the novel. Though she remains unnamed, in his keynote address for a Gileadean Studies symposium in the year 2197, Professor Pieixoto speculates that she might be the same woman who recorded the tapes known collectively as "The Handmaid's Tale."

Professor Maryanne Crescent Moon A scholar of Gileadean Studies. Professor Crescent Moon chairs the Thirteenth Symposium for Gileadean Studies, which takes place in the year 2197.

Professor James Darcy Pieixoto A scholar of Gileadean Studies. Professor Pieixoto delivers the keynote lecture at the Thirteenth Symposium for Gileadean Studies in 2197. He speaks about the authenticity of "The Ardua Hall Holograph," as well as the transcripts of the two testimonies given by Agnes (Witness 369A) and Daisy (Witness 369B).

ANALYSIS OF MAJOR CHARACTERS

AUNT LYDIA

Margaret Atwood originally introduced Aunt Lydia in her earlier novel, *The Handmaid's Tale*, in which the character seemed fully aligned with Gilead's oppressive policies against women. *The Testaments* offers a contrasting view. Prior to the coup that overthrew the United States government and established the Republic of Gilead, Aunt Lydia enjoyed a successful career as a judge. After the transition of power, she became one of four elite women charged by Commander Judd with founding the Aunts, an autonomous order that was to preside over the laws and regulations governing Gilead's women. Over the course of *The Testaments*, Aunt Lydia reveals the horrifying conditions that led her to join the ranks of Gilead's elite. She also explains how she has leveraged the power of her top position. Though no longer officially a judge, Aunt Lydia continues to administer justice in whatever ways she can. She also uses her power to gather evidence against Gilead's authorities and to plot the regime's downfall from within. Ultimately, the transformation that Aunt Lydia undergoes in *The Testaments* has less to do with a change in her character and more to do with a change in the reader's perception of her.

As one of three narrators in the novel, Aunt Lydia records the story of her rise to power in a manuscript known as "The Ardua Hall Holograph." Despite claiming that she joined Gilead mainly in order to survive and subvert the regime, Aunt Lydia by no means presents herself as a saint. In her manuscript, she frequently expresses her anxiety about what her unknown future reader will think of her. Aunt Lydia recognizes that her working methods have sometimes proven morally suspect. She may have labored for a good cause, but her efforts have also contributed to a great deal of suffering and even death. In addition to sacrificing individuals in service to her larger goals, she has also found no small amount of personal pleasure in manipulating others and turning them against each other. Aunt Lydia will go to virtually any lengths to get what she wants, and she finds her substantial power intoxicating. At one point, she even doubts her strength to remain committed to her cause and not give in to the allure of even greater power. In the end, the reader must judge whether Aunt Lydia's contributions to the greater good outweigh the harm she has caused.

AGNES JEMIMA

Agnes grew up in the prominent household of Commander Kyle. Though she benefited from the loving care of her adoptive mother, Tabitha, from a young age, Agnes secretly harbored doubts about Gilead's treatment of women. She grew increasingly disenchanted after she survived a traumatic sexual assault and witnessed the horrific death of her family's Handmaid, Ofkyle, during child-birth. Depressed, Agnes flouted her betrothal to the high-ranking Commander Judd and pledged as a Supplicant in the order of the Aunts. Agnes's time at Ardua Hall transformed her. There she reunited with her old classmate, Becka, who quickly became like a sister to her. She also learned that the Aunts derived their power by collecting other people's secrets, and she felt tanta-lized by this promise of power and security. Agnes's life changed course again when Daisy arrived at Ardua Hall, and Aunt Lydia informed her that Daisy was "Baby Nicole" and that they were sisters. Aunt Lydia also asked Agnes to participate in a plot to, as she described it, reform Gilead's corrupt core. Agnes chose to give up the power that life as an Aunt had promised and instead found a different kind of power in her new relationship to her sister and her commitment to a just cause.

DAISY

Daisy grew up believing that she was an ordinary Canadian girl. She had a supportive, if somewhat distant, relationship with her parents. Soon after she decided, against her parents' wishes, to attend a rally against Gilead's human rights violations, Daisy's world fell apart and she was forced to undergo a series of rapid transformations, from disenchanted orphan to reluctant revo-lutionary to hero. When her parents were suddenly murdered, a group of Mayday operatives working to take Gilead down informed her that her parents were, in fact, not her parents and that she was "Baby Nicole," a child who had attained legendary status after getting smuggled out of Gilead. The Mayday operatives who took Daisy into their care persuaded her to participate in a dangerous plan to infiltrate Gilead and retrieve a cache of top-secret documents from an anonymous, high-ranking source. Despite initially feeling reluctant about her participation in the mission, Daisy made it into Gilead, and the key role she played getting the documents back out demonstrated her bravery and fortitude. Perhaps more important than her successful infiltration and escape was the new relationship she forged with a Gileadean woman named Agnes, who turned out to be her sister. Not long after losing the only parents she'd ever known, Daisy ends the novel by finding a renewed sense of belonging with her sister and biological mother.

Themes, Motifs & Symbols

Themes

Themes are the fundamental and often universal ideas explored in a literary work.

Power

The narrators of *The Testaments* contend with the allure of power in a society that otherwise disempowers women. Prior to the coup that established Gilead, Aunt Lydia enjoyed the power and prestige that accompanied her work as a judge. Though she lost this power upon her arrest, Aunt Lydia quickly rose in Gilead's ranks to become the most powerful of the four founding Aunts. Aunt Lydia wanted to use her power to topple Gilead. However, she also enjoyed the privileges that power brought her, and she worried that her all-too-human vulnerability to the allure of power would tempt her to abandon her life's plan of bringing down the regime. As someone who learned early in life just how powerless Gileadean women were, Agnes felt tantalized by the power wielded by the Aunts. When she realized that Aunts got their power from collecting other people's secrets, she envisioned an intoxicating future in which she could take vengeance on those who had wronged her. Daisy proves comparatively more reluctant to embrace the power she possesses as Baby Nicole, but she ultimately uses that power to help take Gilead down.

The Collective Nature of Guilt

The Testaments emphasizes how guilt is not simply a matter of individual actions but of societal complacency. The novel explores this theme in terms of gender. Though men controlled Gilead, the regime used certain women's participation in the patriarchy to lend it a form of legitimacy. The four founding Aunts collaborated with Commander Judd to establish oppressive new laws to restrict women's freedoms and govern every aspect of their life. Likewise, some upper-class women adapted to their new lives by innovating fresh ways to assert their dominance over other women, particularly Handmaids. These women are, in their own way, guilty of collectively supporting Gilead's theocratic regime. A more explicit example of collective guilt arises when Commander Judd tests Aunt Lydia's loyalty by coercing her to participate in an execution of other women. After the event, Commander Judd claims that the rifle Aunt Lydia used had a blank in it rather than a bullet. Though he says this to relieve her sense of guilt for killing another woman (and inspire loyalty in her), Aunt Lydia understands that her intention to kill had already condemned her even if her action caused no direct harm. Thus, any individual who either directly or indirectly contributed to Gilead's survival shares in the society's collective guilt.

UNCERTAINTY

The question of what the future will bring resonates throughout much of *The Testaments*. The novel's major conflict centers on Gilead's oppression of women and their consequent desire to topple the patriarchal regime to secure a better, freer future. Each of the three narrators worries about the attainability of such a future. Aunt Lydia frequently meditates on the uncertainty of her plan's success and on the strength of her own commitment. She also frets over whether her unknown future reader will believe her to be a monster. More than anything, though, she fears the possibility that Gilead will remain intact for the next thousand years. Agnes's and Daisy's stories go some way to balance Aunt Lydia's uncertainty. Whereas Aunt Lydia composes her manuscript not knowing what will happen in the future, the young women offer retrospective accounts that indicate the eventual success of their mission. Despite this formal aspect of the novel's structure, both Agnes and Daisy recount moments of profound loss and disillusionment in their youth, which led to feelings of confusion and hopelessness. However, despite their uncertainty, all three women committed themselves to a vision of a better world at great personal risk.

MOTIFS

> *Motifs are recurring structures, contrasts, or literary devices that can help to develop and inform the text's major themes.*

EMBROIDERY

Crafts are used as a socially acceptable form of creative expression for women in Gilead. When young upper-class women attend a school that prepares them for married life, they learn all sorts of domestic crafts to signal a Wife's virtue. However, in contrast to other crafts, embroidery carries a subversive significance throughout *The Testaments*. For instance, as she waited for the Aunts to arrange her marriage, Agnes embroidered a skull. Although the skull was a traditional symbol within Christian iconography, it carried a secret meaning for Agnes, who embroidered it in order to curse Paula. Thus, under cover of embroidery's virtue, Agnes expressed her hatred for a cruel woman. Embroidery's subversive possibilities arise again when Agnes learns to read and write, two skills Gilead's patriarchy considers dangerous for women. When Agnes has trouble with writing, Becka says that writing is just like embroidery, suggesting that the well-regarded domestic craft may carry an intrinsic danger to Gilead. Finally, Aunt Lydia concludes her manuscript with a reference to a famous phrase that Mary, Queen of Scots embroidered just before she was executed for plotting to assassinate Queen Elizabeth I. Likening embroidery to political intrigue, Aunt Lydia writes: "Such excellent embroiderers, women are."

ESCAPE

Women try every method possible to escape Gilead and its oppressive regime. Many attempt physical escapes, moving along the Underground Femaleroad toward Canada. In Part VII, Aunt Lydia admits that Gilead has "an embarrassingly high emigration rate," and the reader sees evidence of this throughout the novel. Agnes and Daisy's mother managed a successful escape. Others who have less success, such as Paula's Handmaid, are caught and executed for treason. The restriction of women's freedoms that drives Gilead's women to flee physically also causes them to attempt other methods of escape, namely suicide. The issue of suicide arises frequently in *The Testaments*. Becka, for instance, tries to kill herself in order to avoid having to get married. Agnes also contemplates suicide to evade the trauma of a forced marriage. Other examples include Shunammite's reference to a Handmaid who drank drain cleaner and Becka's story of Aunt Lily's suicide. The motif of escape threaded throughout *The Testaments* underscores the horrific circumstances that drive many Gileadean women to seek a way out regardless of the cost.

APHORISMS

Gileadeans frequently use aphorisms in everyday speech, which indicates the unreflective and rote nature of their beliefs. The first usage of aphorisms occurs when Ada, a Mayday operative who grew up in Gilead, casually mutters to Daisy, "Least said, soonest mended." Aunt Lydia says the same phrase in the novel's next section, suggesting the commonness of the formulaic expression throughout Gilead. In a few instances, Aunt Lydia comments indirectly on the use of aphorisms in Gilead. For instance, in Part III, she describes the Latin saying that she herself made up to serve as the official motto for Ardua Hall: *Per Ardua Cum Estrus*. She doesn't fully define the motto for the reader, but she does note that the words she used to compose it have multiple, contradictory meanings. As such, none of the women who utter the motto on a daily basis have a firm grasp of what it really means. Aunt Lydia relishes the irony of believers uttering expressions of belief they don't actually understand, as it highlights the shaky foundation and weak-mindedness of the regime. The frequent use of aphorisms in Gilead thus demonstrates a widespread willingness to mindlessly follow authority.

Symbols

Symbols are objects, characters, figures, or colors used to represent abstract ideas or concepts.

Agnes's Dollhouse

The luxury dollhouse that Agnes played with as a girl symbolizes Gilead's traditional social hierarchy. The set included several dolls: a Commander, a Wife, a Martha, a Handmaid, and an Aunt. Taken collectively, the set reproduced Gileadean society in miniature. Despite being a toy, the set functioned as a tool for indoctrinating young girls, ensuring that they would accept Gileadean social and gender roles as normal. By playing with the different dolls, girls would practice everyday social relations until they came to seem natural. In Agnes's case, however, the dollhouse did not function as a tool for replicating Gilead's normative social dynamics. Instead, she played with her dolls according to her own rules. For instance, instead of imagining the Commander doll as a masculine, commanding figure, Agnes modeled him after her own father, a quiet and distant man who retreated into his study. Agnes also enjoyed locking the Aunt doll in the cellar, and she positioned the Martha doll nearby, pretending not to hear the Aunt doll's cries for help. Even though the dollhouse was intended to indoctrinate her, Agnes turned it into a tool for imaginative subversion, foreshadowing how she will subvert the regime later in life.

Baby Nicole

Although Baby Nicole is a real person, her fame and status both inside and outside of Gilead turned her into a symbol with competing meanings. The story of Baby Nicole caused a scandal about fifteen years prior to the events that lead to Gilead's collapse. At the time, Gilead had a problem with women trying to escape to Canada. The most infamous case involved a Handmaid who successfully crossed the border with a baby that legally belonged to a prominent Commander. This baby was Baby Nicole. Many outside of Gilead celebrated the successful escape and saw Baby Nicole as a symbol of triumph over oppression. In Gilead, however, Aunt Lydia and the Commanders used Baby Nicole as a propaganda tool to spark the fire of nationalism. They wanted the people of Gilead to see Baby Nicole as a symbol of the outside world's cruelty. If Gileadeans felt victimized, then their allegiance to the regime would grow in kind. Baby Nicole's competing symbolic meanings come to a head when Daisy learns that she's really Baby Nicole. As a young person with an interest in social justice, she ultimately chooses to leverage her legendary status against the very regime that created it.

The Story of the Concubine

The biblical story that Aunt Vidala tells Agnes and her classmates about a concubine symbolizes how Gilead's regime uses censorship as a tool for oppression. Vidala's story tells of a concubine who runs away from her master. The man tracks her down, and as they journey back to the man's house, lustful local men try to attack the man, who puts the concubine in front of them instead. She is raped and killed. Much later, when she joins the Aunts and learns to read the Bible on her own, Agnes learns that Aunt Vidala had left out the part where the man cuts the murdered concubine into twelve pieces, sends each to one of the twelve Tribes of Israel, and starts a war between them. Aunt Vidala's censored version of the story attempted to make the violence against the concubine seem justified. In retrospect, however, Agnes understands that Aunt Vidala had intentionally modified the story to scare her pupils into submission and warn them of what happens to disobedient women. This recognition inspires a crisis of faith that leads Agnes to distrust the story of Gilead's exceptional status.

SUMMARY & ANALYSIS

PARTS I–II

SUMMARY: PART I: STATUE

The Testaments opens with a document titled "The Ardua Hall Holograph," written in the first person by a woman whom we later learn is Aunt Lydia. The narrator describes a ceremony that occurred nine years prior to honor her achievements and reveal a statue of her likeness. Her colleague and enemy, Aunt Vidala, grudgingly presided over the ceremony.

The statue is larger than life, and it depicts the narrator as a younger woman in a strong, confident stance, looking far away toward "some cosmic point of reference understood to represent my idealism, my unflinching commitment to duty." The statue also includes two other figures: a Handmaid and a Pearl Girl. In the nine years since its creation, the statue has weathered. Devotees have taken to placing eggs, oranges, croissants, and other offerings at the statue's feet.

The narrator directly addresses her unknown future reader and expresses concern about the risk she runs by writing this manuscript. She's writing her testimony in a private room in the Ardua Hall library. She confesses that she has spilled her share of blood in service to Gilead's reigning regime, which seeks to prepare the way for a "morally pure generation" to come.

SUMMARY: PART II: PRECIOUS FLOWER

Part II shifts to a new narrator named Agnes Jemima, who gives testimony about what it was like to grow up within Gilead. Her narrative is entitled "Transcript of Witness Testimony 369A."

Agnes belonged to an elite family, which meant she was destined to marry a Commander. Her privilege enabled her to attend a special school run by the strict Aunt Vidala and the comparatively gentle Aunt Estée. Aunt Vidala taught that all girls were "precious flowers" and needed to be kept safe from the ravenous men of the world. By contrast, Aunt Estée insisted that some men were decent and that when it came time for the girls to marry, the Aunts would help choose one of the decent ones.

Agnes enjoyed a loving relationship with her mother, Tabitha, who liked to tell a fantastical story about how she chose Agnes from a group of girls locked in an enchanted castle. Every night they sang a prayer about angels keeping watch over them. The prayer soothed Agnes, but it also made her wonder about the difference between biblical angels and the armed guards called "Angels."

Together with Tabitha, Agnes played with a deluxe dollhouse set that included several dolls. She made the Commander doll act quiet and distant like her own father, Commander Kyle. Agnes left the Handmaid doll in the box since Handmaids made her nervous. Though she didn't know what Handmaids did, she suspected they took part in "something damaging, or something damaged." The dollhouse set also came with an Aunt doll, which Agnes kept locked in the cellar. The Martha doll pretended not to hear when the Aunt doll cried for help.

Agnes explains that her second name, Jemima, came from the story of Job. According to the Bible, Job lost his children when God tested him. When Job passed the test, God gave him new children, one of whom was named Jemima. Agnes wondered why Job would accept the replacement children and forget about the dead ones.

Tabitha grew ill, and when she was resting, Agnes spent time with her household's three Marthas: Vera, Rosa, and Zilla. The Marthas refused to let Agnes help them in their duties. They thought she needed to prepare herself to become a Wife, in which position she would preside over her own Marthas. They did let her play with scraps of dough. Agnes liked to fashion dough men since eating them gave her a sense of power.

At school, Agnes's peers included Becka and Shunammite. Becka was shy and quiet. By contrast, Shunammite was brash and belligerent. She claimed to be Agnes's best friend, but Agnes suspected her of social climbing since Shunammite's father wasn't as prominent as Commander Kyle. Shunammite had learned from her Martha that Agnes's mother was dying. The rumor upset Agnes, who insisted that Tabitha was merely sick.

ANALYSIS: PARTS I–II

The Testaments is the sequel to Margaret Atwood's 1985 novel *The Handmaid's Tale*, and anyone who has read the earlier novel will instantly recognize the first narrator as a woman living in the Republic of Gilead. For such readers, the Handmaid depicted in the statue will recall the previous novel's chilling story of Offred, who navigated the terrifying coup that transformed the United States into a theocratic regime ruled by a patriarchal elite known as the Sons of Jacob. Under the dystopian government of Gilead, the sphere of women had its own hierarchy. Aunts stood at the top, presiding over the legal and religious ideology regulating all women in Gilead's society. Below them stood Wives, the most elite of whom were married to high-ranking Commanders. Wives presided over the other women in their homes. Households of prominent Commanders had servants known as Marthas, who did the cooking and cleaning. Below all others stood the Handmaids, a subclass of women whose only official value in an increasingly barren society was their ability to conceive children. Stripped of her identity and referred to by derivatives of her Commander's name, a Handmaid bore her master's children while often suffering the jealous hatred of his Wife.

The manuscript called "The Ardua Hall Holograph" opens with the description of a statue that symbolizes female power. The reader does not yet know whom the statue memorializes, but it's clear that the woman holds a place of privilege. More specifically, she's likely a prominent Aunt, as suggested by the way the figure in the statue presides over a Handmaid and a so-called Pearl Girl. The offerings her admirers place at the statue's feet all honor specifically female attributes. The eggs symbolize fertility, the oranges symbolize pregnancy, and the croissants symbolize the moon, which is traditionally gendered female. Yet for all these symbols of her power, the narrator primes the reader to wonder just how worthy of honor she really is. The statue itself is nine years old and significantly weathered, suggesting that time may also have worn down the confident idealism depicted in her younger self. Furthermore, it is unclear how the viewer should understand her relationship to the other two women included in the sculpture. Does she stand over them in a relationship of collective empowerment, or does she use her power to subjugate them? The ambiguity of female power enshrined in the statue sets the tone for "The Ardua Hall Holograph."

The first narrator's concern about the risks of writing indicates how her manuscript poses a twofold threat. On the one hand, her manuscript poses a specific political threat. The confessional tone with which she concludes Part I implies that she writes for the sake of posterity. That is, she has a story to tell about her own actions that, though perhaps distasteful for her future reader, will nonetheless shed light on her own efforts to subvert the Republic of Gilead. On the other hand, her manuscript poses a more general social threat. Anyone who has previously read *The Handmaid's Tale* knows that Gilead's male leadership has forbidden all women from reading and writing. The only women who retain these privileges are Aunts, who only gain access to the library after receiving an intensive education that ensures their unwavering support of the ruling ideology. In summary, the fact that a woman is writing this manuscript seems dangerous enough, and the fact that an Aunt might be writing against the regime may well prove revolutionary.

Despite enjoying a happy childhood in Gilead, the novel's second narrator, Agnes Jemima, harbored heretical thoughts from an early age. For example, the deluxe dollhouse her mother gave her was clearly designed as a tool for the ideological indoctrination of young girls. The set implicitly reinforced the traditional social hierarchy within the elite Gilead home by including a Commander, a Wife, a Martha, a Handmaid, and an Aunt. Yet the way Agnes played with her dolls demonstrates an innate distrust of the traditional domestic hierarchy. She removed the Handmaid from circulation altogether. She also reversed the usual hierarchy of power among women. Instead of presiding over other women, the Aunt doll got locked in the cellar, begging the unsympathetic Martha doll to let her out. Agnes's active imagination clearly subverted Gilead's social norms. Agnes also challenged Gilead's religious ideology when she learned the origin of her second name, Jemima. In the Bible, Jemima was the name of one of the children God gave Job after he lost his original children in one of God's moral tests. Agnes wondered why Job accepted the new children instead of revolting against God's cruelty. These heretical thoughts foreshadow her eventual break with Gilead.

PARTS III–IV

SUMMARY: PART III: HYMN

I've become swollen with power, true, but also nebulous with it—formless, shape-shifting. I am everywhere and nowhere: even in the minds of the Commanders I cast an unsettling shadow. How can I regain myself? How to shrink back to my normal size, the size of an ordinary woman?

(See QUOTATIONS, *p. 68*)

SUMMARY & ANALYSIS

The author of "The Ardua Hall Holograph" reflects on the appearance of her aging body. She explains that she used to be "handsome," but now the best word to describe her look would be "imposing." She also wonders how her story will end. She wonders whether she'll die of old age, or if the state will execute her. She recognizes that she still has some choice in how she'll die, which is "freedom of a sort."

Once again addressing the reader, the narrator explicitly reveals her identity as Aunt Lydia, a legendary figure who serves as a "model of moral perfection," yet has become tainted by power. She also notes that before Gilead, she was a family court judge.

Aunt Lydia writes this installment on Easter. She describes the meal the Aunts shared at Ardua Hall, where she saw Aunt Elizabeth take one more egg than her share. She also describes how she led the Prayer of Grace, which ends with a motto she wrote herself: *Per Ardua Cum Estrus*. It brings her pleasure that the other Aunts don't know for sure what the motto means but that they nonetheless repeat the words piously.

Aunt Lydia notes how she has used the figure known as Baby Nicole as a propaganda tool. Baby Nicole is the name of an infant who, many years prior, was successfully smuggled out of Gilead and into Canada. Ever since that infamous event, Aunt Lydia has mobilized Baby Nicole's image in various ways to manipulate the emotions of people in Gilead. Aunt Lydia remarks that Baby Nicole still has "a brilliant future."

After the Easter meal, she retreated into the depths of the library. She has a private inner sanctum there with a small personal library of forbidden books as well as a set of files containing the secret histories of Gilead. It is in this sanctum that Aunt Lydia composes her manuscript, which she keeps hidden inside a copy of Cardinal Newman's *Apologia Pro Vita Sua*, meaning "A Defense of One's Life." She reflects on the appropriateness of the book's title. Like Cardinal Newman, she is writing to defend her life.

SUMMARY: PART IV: THE CLOTHES HOUND

Part IV shifts to a new narrator named Daisy, who is giving testimony about her involvement in "this whole story." Her narrative is entitled "Transcript of Witness Testimony 369B." Daisy begins her story just before what she thought was her sixteenth birthday, around the time she discovered that everything in her life was a lie.

Her parents, Melanie and Neil, owned and operated a used clothing store called The Clothes Hound in Toronto, Canada. Melanie
worked the sales floor and managed inventory, and Neil did the
accounting. Neil also collected a variety of objects on shelves in
his office, and he had a special interest in cameras. He also kept a
mysterious object in his safe, which Daisy thought was a toy but
never got to play with. Daisy spent virtually all of her free time helping out in the store since Melanie worried about her staying in the
house alone.

In addition to customers, several other types frequented the store.
Street people sometimes came in to use the restroom. A middle-aged
woman named Ada also visited often. Melanie claimed she was a
close friend, but Daisy found it suspicious that Ada always arrived in
a different car. Finally, silver-clad missionaries from Gilead—known
as "Pearl Girls"—occasionally came in to deliver brochures. Many of
these brochures featured images and slogans related to Baby Nicole.

Melanie and Neil were different from other parents. For one
thing, they had no photographs of Daisy growing up. For another,
they were overprotective. Just before her sixteenth birthday, Daisy
attended an assembly protesting Gilead's human rights violations
against her parents' wishes. At first, the protest thrilled her, but when
skirmishes broke out, she tried to flee. Ada found her in the crowd
and escorted her home, where she saw herself on the news.

Three days later, there was a break-in at The Clothes Hound, and
Neil said the thieves had taken an old camera. That night, the news
reported on a Pearl Girl known as Aunt Adrianna, who was found
dead, hanging from a doorknob in a condo.

On the day of her birthday, Daisy went to school as usual. But at
the end of the day, Ada appeared to pick her up instead of Melanie
and explained that Daisy's parents had both died from a car bomb
planted outside their store.

ANALYSIS: PARTS III–IV

In the second part of her manuscript, the author of "The Ardua
Hall Holograph" reveals herself as Aunt Lydia. Readers of *The
Handmaid's Tale* will know that Aunt Lydia featured prominently
in that novel as one of the most formidable and dangerous female
representatives of Gilead's theocratic regime. Aunt Lydia made many
misogynist statements that showed her to be complicit in sustain-
ing the patriarchal system of male dominance. Offred, the protagonist of the earlier novel, had special contempt for Aunt Lydia, who

compelled her to go through a traumatic process of "re-education." However, now that Aunt Lydia speaks from her own point of view, her character begins to take on a different appearance. Whereas in *The Handmaid's Tale* the reader only ever viewed Aunt Lydia through the eyes of others, her first-person narrative in *The Testaments* promises to provide a behind-the-scenes account of her own experience. Even if such an account may not exonerate her of her crimes, it may help explain the reasons for her involvement with Gilead's ruling class and the actions she's performed on its behalf.

Aunt Lydia presents herself as a woman who wields great power, and already the reader can discern some of the sources of her power. For one thing, she takes pleasure in her ability to manipulate others. When she turned the story of Baby Nicole into propaganda, she demonstrated her significant influence over the hearts and minds of everyday people in Gilead. Yet Aunt Lydia's ability to manipulate others does not always serve the interests of the Gileadean regime. For instance, she clearly relishes the confusion that her Latin motto causes her fellow Aunts. In this case, her manipulation has a subversive effect, since the Aunts' blind display of piety demonstrates how statements of faith in Gilead are often only skin-deep. Stated differently, Aunt Lydia shows that her fellow Aunts either don't believe what they say, or that they don't understand their own beliefs. As the example of the Latin motto shows, Aunt Lydia has a leg up on others, in large part because she knows more than they do. She collects secrets about other people's behavior, both through her own observations and through a network of surveillance equipment and informants. As a former judge, Aunt Lydia is symbolically poised to gather evidence and pass judgment.

When Aunt Lydia declares that she possesses "freedom of a sort," she points to the ambiguous nature of the choices she has had to make throughout her life. As a woman living under a male-dominated regime, Aunt Lydia's options have been strictly limited. Yet whatever constraints others may have placed on her, she also recognizes that she has never fully lost the power to make choices. Given the nature of her restrictions, those choices have not always been easy to make or to stomach. Even so, she made her own choices and wishes to take responsibility for them, provided that she has an opportunity to clarify the context in which she made them. To give a sense of the high stakes involved in her decision-making, Aunt Lydia describes how she possesses the dubious "freedom" to choose how she will die. Either she can continue to write her manuscript and risk a horrific execution at the hands of the state, or she can stay silent and die of old age. The former path entails great personal suffering but for a greater cause. The latter path ensures relative personal comfort, but the betrayal of her personal beliefs.

Daisy's narrative introduces a new kind of genre to *The Testaments*: that of the thriller. The other two narrators' accounts read like memoirs. Aunt Lydia's narrative reads like a confessional memoir, and Agnes's narrative reads like a coming-of-age memoir. By contrast, Daisy's account of how she became involved in "this whole story" uses foreshadowing to add tension and plant clues about false identities, foreign spies, and covert revolutionary operatives. Daisy begins her story by telling the reader how she found out her whole life was a "fraud." Although she is not specific about what she means by this, Daisy offers several clues that the facts of her life didn't quite add up. Her parents, for instance, struck her as oddly overprotective, and the lack of photographs of her as a child also seemed suspicious. She mentions a mysterious object in Neil's safe, which we later learn is a covert communication device. In Neil's office, there's also a poster that reads "Loose lips sink ships." The poster is a piece of World War II–era paraphernalia urging people to hold their secrets close, and it foreshadows the revelation that Neil and Melanie are both operatives in the covert revolutionary group known as Mayday.

PARTS V–VI

SUMMARY: PART V: VAN

Aunt Lydia speculates on who her future reader might be. She assumes her future reader will wonder how she has avoided being found out and executed by Gilead's male ruling class. She attributes her political longevity to three facts. First, as the leader of the Aunts, she controls the women's cultural sphere of Gilead. Second, she has collected a lot of dirt on those in power. Finally, she's discreet and patiently waits for opportunities to use her power.

Aunt Lydia describes a meeting she had with Commander Judd the day before. Commander Judd controls the intelligence agency known as the Eyes and hence wields great power and influence in Gilead. He works closely with Aunt Lydia, who knows he has discreetly killed several of his wives in order to marry ever-younger women.

Commander Judd informed Aunt Lydia that agents of the Eyes in Canada killed two of the most active Mayday operatives, based on valuable information provided by Pearl Girls. Aunt Lydia notes that she came up with the Pearl Girls missionary program at a time when many Gilead women were successfully escaping to Canada. However, Commander Judd took credit for the Pearl Girls idea, which saved his political reputation. At the end of their meeting, Commander Judd expressed concern that the Canadian Mayday operatives must have been in contact with someone in Gilead.

Aunt Lydia writes of her regret at not having escaped before the coup that established Gilead, but then dismisses such regret as being of no practical use. She then begins an account of her experience during the coup. Shortly after the Sons of Jacob "liquidated" the U.S. Congress, armed men came to the office where she worked as a judge. The men arrested all of the women there, and they ordered Aunt Lydia and her colleague Anita to be sent to a nearby stadium.

SUMMARY: PART VI: SIX FOR DEAD

Agnes's testimony picks up following the death of her mother, Tabitha. At the funeral, Agnes spoke with a recent widow named Paula, whose husband's death had inspired gossip. Paula claimed that their Handmaid had accidentally killed her husband. However, another version circulating among Marthas held that Paula's husband had made illicit sexual demands on the Handmaid, who had killed him for revenge. Agnes preferred the second version, and she liked to imagine Paula kneeling in a pool of her late husband's blood. Not long after the funeral, Agnes's father married Paula.

Around that time, a disturbing event occurred at school. Aunt Vidala told Agnes's class the story of "the Concubine Cut into Twelve Pieces," in which a man's concubine runs away. The man finds her at the house of her father, who agrees to give her back to the man. As they journey home, lustful men come to assault the man, but instead of facing the angry mob himself, the man throws the concubine out of the house. Agnes later learned the part of the story Aunt Vidala left out, in which the man cuts the concubine's body into twelve pieces, sends one to each of the twelve Tribes of Israel, and starts a war between them. But even without the full story, the story disturbed the girls. Becka, in particular, felt horrified by the injustice in the story and claimed that she'd never get married.

Around the same time, Agnes was entering puberty and grew concerned about her changing body. In anticipation of getting her first period, she felt like her body was a minefield. One day, she went to see the dentist, Dr. Grove, who happened to be Becka's father. During the appointment, Dr. Grove sexually molested Agnes. She felt defiled and believed Paula knew what might happen at the dentist's office, but she didn't tell anybody.

At school, Shunammite spread rumors that Tabitha wasn't Agnes's biological mother and that her real mom was a Handmaid who had tried to smuggle her out of Gilead. Agnes felt that this story must be true. Anxious about her status as "the daughter of a slut," Agnes prayed to Aunt Lydia.

A Handmaid joined the household to conceive Commander Kyle's baby. The Handmaid, known as Ofkyle, eventually became pregnant and carried the child to full term. When the day came for Ofkyle to give birth, a medical complication arose, and a male physician performed an operation that saved the baby but killed the Handmaid. Traumatized, Agnes promised never to forget Ofkyle, whose real name, she learned later, was Crystal. At the Handmaid's modest funeral, Agnes fumed silently at the injustice of her death.

ANALYSIS: PARTS V–VI

Aunt Lydia's meeting with Commander Judd clearly demonstrates the considerable nature of the power she holds in Gilead. Despite appearing to take a subservient role, Aunt Lydia shows the extent to which Commander Judd's reputation rests on initiatives that she created. For instance, she was the one to design and implement the Pearl Girls missionary initiative, which aimed to draw domestic and international attention away from the large numbers of fugitive women escaping from Gilead to Canada. The Pearl Girls program succeeded, and Commander Judd took credit for its success. In this way, Aunt Lydia exposes for her reader the basic fact that Commander Judd owed her his good reputation, which provided her with some security. And just as Aunt Lydia's ingenuity propped Commander Judd up, her knowledge of his darkest secrets made it possible for her to bring him down at any time. She convinces him that she's on his side by helping him to disguise the murders of his wives but harbors an ulterior motive that she does not yet reveal. Aunt Lydia wields her power skillfully and quietly, waiting for the right moment to pounce.

Agnes continues to showcase her heretical imagination when she discusses the competing stories about the death of Paula's husband. In Part II, Agnes described her unconventional ways of playing with her dollhouse set. From a young age, she used her imagination to subvert Gilead's orthodox ideas about the organization of a household. Some years later, following the death of her beloved mother figure, Tabitha, Agnes once again shows herself capable of unorthodox thoughts. Agnes recounts two different stories about how Paula's husband died. The official story, as told by Paula, had a simple and undramatic narrative that treated the man's death as an unfortunate accident. But the alternative story, transmitted by gossipy servants, introduced elements of intrigue, betrayal, and gruesome violence into the otherwise bland official account. Attracted to good storytelling, Agnes strongly preferred the latter narrative, which fed her imagination with violent ideas of a female's revenge on her male oppressor. In particular, the enjoyment Agnes found in picturing Paula kneeling in a pool of her husband's body shows her natural capacity to think outside the confines of official Gilead ideology.

Agnes took a further step toward discovering the moral rottenness of Gilead as she reached puberty and saw how her changing body brought unwanted attention. From an early age, Agnes learned in the Vidala School that her body was a source of sin. She also learned that any inappropriate male attention to her body would reflect negatively on her, not the men. As such, when puberty hit and Agnes began to notice changes in her body, she feared that bad things would start happening to her. Agnes learned just how dangerous and unavoidable this minefield of her body was during an appointment with Dr. Grove, her family dentist. Dr. Grove had a good local reputation, even though some girls at school gossiped about his being a "pervert." However, Agnes knew to respect his male authority. For this reason, she felt paralyzed and powerless when, in the middle of her appointment, he began to grope her. The experience traumatized her, not least because she felt unable to report the incident since she assumed she would be blamed. Though she felt too confused at the time, the older Agnes now understands this incident as a sign of Gilead's moral corruption as the state protected a pedophile.

Agnes approached a breaking point when she personally witnessed the injustice perpetrated against her family's Handmaid, Ofkyle. Prior to Ofkyle's arrival in the house, Agnes knew little about who Handmaids were or what duties they performed. They unnerved her, and she even refused to play with her Handmaid doll. But Agnes came to learn more about Handmaids and their role in Gileadean society once Ofkyle came to conceive Commander Judd's child. Significantly, Ofkyle's arrival roughly coincided with Agnes learning that her own biological mother was a Handmaid. At first, the news terrified and depressed her. Most people in Gilead thought of Handmaids as "sluts," and as such, Agnes couldn't help but think badly of her real mother. But her mind changed when she witnessed how Ofkyle was used as a breeding machine, then cruelly sacrificed and summarily disposed of and forgotten. Agnes understood that her own mother might have suffered similar injustices. This realization helped Agnes begin to see the systematic subordination of Handmaids. Although she didn't yet take the further step to link this subordination with Gilead's state-sanctioned violence against women in general, Agnes's outrage about Ofkyle and her mother does foreshadow her eventual willingness to join a plot against Gilead.

PARTS VII–VIII

SUMMARY: PART VII: STADIUM

Aunt Lydia writes that Gilead has "an embarrassingly high emigration rate" for a nation that claims to be "God's kingdom." The vast rural areas of Maine and Vermont pose challenges for security, since the people who live in those areas remain hostile to the government of Gilead. She explains that Aunts Elizabeth, Helen, and Vidala recently formulated an official plan for ending "the female emigrant problem." Earlier in the day, these Aunts came to visit her to report about raids on various heretics, including supporters of the Underground Femaleroad. Aunt Lydia accepted the news cheerfully and then informed the other Aunts of the existence of a possible spy in Gilead, maybe even in Ardua Hall.

Aunt Lydia returns to the story of her arrest. Guards drove her and Anita to a stadium, then herded them to a section of bleachers reserved for women with legal training. Waiting in the bleachers, Aunt Lydia took stock of her situation. As an overachieving "smarty-pants girl" who had grown up in a family that rejected education, she had developed grit and perseverance. She would have to put both to use again.

Late in the afternoon, armed men led a procession of blindfolded women onto the field and executed them. Aunt Lydia wondered why the men would bother with such a spectacle if they planned to murder all of the women.

SUMMARY: PART VIII: CARNARVON

Still in shock after learning about the deaths of Melanie and Neil, Daisy agreed to follow Ada's lead. Ada drove her to a Quaker meeting house, which turned out to be an outpost of SanctuCare, an organization that supported refugees from Gilead. Ada left Daisy there for a while, and Daisy watched as volunteers tried to comfort crying refugees. At the time, she wondered why the women cried now that they were safe, but she explains that her own later experience helped her understand they cried from the release of stress.

An hour later, Ada returned and instructed Daisy to change into clothes that would disguise her. They got back into the gray van, and Ada drove them to an old mansion on the outskirts of Toronto. Inside, Ada showed Daisy to a furnished room. She brought Daisy food and chocolate cake for her birthday, but anxiety kept Daisy from eating.

Daisy woke up the next morning feeling disoriented and thinking about Melanie and Neil. She went into the living room, where Ada was waiting with a middle-aged man named Elijah. Elijah explained to Daisy that the previous day was not her real birthday and that Melanie and Neil weren't her biological parents. He told Daisy that her real parents were still alive and well hidden. They had worked with the organization known as Mayday to smuggle her out of Gilead when she was a child and then placed her in Melanie and Neil's care for safekeeping. Daisy said the story sounded like that of Baby Nicole, and Elijah told her that she indeed was Baby Nicole.

ANALYSIS: PARTS VII–VIII

Aunt Lydia's discussion of how her colleagues designed a program to end "the female emigrant problem" showcases one of the ways that female leadership in Gilead actively supports the oppression of other women. When Aunts Elizabeth, Helena, and Vidala originally came to her office, Aunt Lydia sensed how proud they were of their efforts to shut down the rural network of rebellious citizens aiding female refugees fleeing Gilead. And when they came into her office again to report the removal of a few more links in the chain known as "the Underground Femaleroad," their pride in their work remained as obvious as ever. Aunt Lydia received the news with apparent cheer, yet she also demonstrated a secret disapproval of their work when she redirected the conversation to the issue of a possible traitor in Gilead and then immediately added that the traitor might be in Ardua Hall. Aunt Lydia attempted to subvert her colleagues' work by using their own tactic against them. That is, she attempted to sow distrust amongst her fellow Aunts and thereby prevent them from achieving their goals.

The information Aunt Lydia provides about her own upbringing sheds light on her personality and her political allegiances. When describing the time she spent trapped in the stadium during the coup that established Gilead, Aunt Lydia notes that her childhood experiences prepared her well to fight through oppression. She was an intellectually ambitious youth, but she felt held back by her parents, who saw no point in pursuing education. Despite their rejection of her ambitions, she developed the fortitude necessary not just to fight her way out of her poor, rural hometown but also to put herself through law school, excel as a lawyer, and eventually become a judge. Aunt Lydia's demonstrated ability to push through obstacles and thrive despite adversity formed the bedrock of her personality, and she knew she would need to build on this foundation to survive in the Republic of Gilead. Significantly, Aunt Lydia's rural upbringing also endowed her with a spirit of independence that continues to influence her political allegiances. Just like the rural Mainers and Vermonters who, as she notes, remain steadfast in their disregard for Gilead's policies, Aunt Lydia clearly works to subvert Gilead's interests.

Daisy's experience in the SanctuCare office foreshadows the end of her narrative, when she too will learn how the accumulation of stress affects an individual's psyche. When she first arrived in the SanctuCare office, Daisy felt confused by the crying refugees from Gilead. Her confusion stemmed from the apparent illogic of having an emotional outburst when you're no longer in danger. As a sheltered Canadian girl, Daisy could not fathom the depths of the damage these refugee women had endured in Gilead. As Daisy reflects in her testimony, however, she herself will later gain first-hand experience of a similar psychological phenomenon. Despite not yet knowing the full extent of Daisy's story, the reader does understand that whatever happens in the rest of the novel, Daisy will undergo some kind of stressful experience. And when she emerges safely on the other side, she will have some kind of emotional release, just like the Gilead refugees. In short, the brief scene in the SanctuCare refugee center foreshadows the successful completion of Daisy's future mission.

PARTS IX–X

SUMMARY: PART IX: THANK TANK

Did I weep? Yes: tears came out of my two visible eyes, my moist weeping human eyes. But I had a third eye, in the middle of my forehead. I could feel it: it was cold, like a stone. It did not weep: it saw. And behind it

someone was thinking: I will get you back for this.
I don't care how long it takes or how much shit I have
to eat in the meantime, but I will do it.

(See QUOTATIONS, p. 69)

Aunt Lydia describes how Commander Judd had summoned her for a meeting earlier in the day. She believes that he considers her "the embodiment of his will." Commander Judd reported that his Wife was suffering some affliction of the internal organs. Aunt Lydia offered to arrange a consultation at the Calm and Balm Clinic at Ardua Hall. Commander Judd declined the offer, and Aunt Lydia suspected that his Wife would die soon, putting him in search of another young bride.

Commander Judd told Aunt Lydia that the Canadian government had officially ruled Aunt Adrianna's death a suicide. Gilead's official response would be that the Canadian government was covering up Mayday terrorist activities. Aunt Lydia praised the official response despite knowing the real story. Aunt Sally, who had served with Aunt Adrianna as a Pearl Girl in Toronto, had come to see her immediately upon returning to Ardua Hall. Aunt Sally had explained that Aunt Adrianna had suddenly attacked her and that she had killed her in self-defense. Aunt Sally also suspected that Melanie and Neil's daughter may have been Baby Nicole. Once she confirmed that Aunt Sally hadn't told anyone else about her experiences in Canada, Aunt Lydia sent her to the Margery Kempe Retreat House, where she would be drugged into oblivion.

Commander Judd explained that the Eyes had discovered among Neil's possessions a microdot camera, an old technology once used to print information on easily concealable microscopic dots. He suspected that someone in Gilead was using the same technology to communicate with Mayday operatives, and Aunt Lydia pledged that they would "outfox Mayday yet."

Aunt Lydia returns to the story of her arrest. She describes the unsanitary conditions of the stadium and its restrooms, which reduced the women to subhuman animals. Each day more women were executed, and one afternoon Aunt Lydia noticed women among those performing the executions. On the sixth night, guards took Anita, and men came for Aunt Lydia the following night. The men escorted her to a former police station, where she met Commander Judd. He asked her if she would cooperate, and she said she couldn't agree without knowing more details.

He ordered her sent to the "Thank Tank" for solitary confinement. After an unknown period of time, men came and beat her.
Sometime later, guards took her from the cell and took her to a
luxury hotel room. She recuperated there for three days, at the end
of which she found laid out for her a garment that she recognized
from seeing it on the female shooters at the stadium. Not knowing
what else to do, she put it on.

SUMMARY: PART X: SPRING GREEN

Agnes describes the preparations leading up to her betrothal. One
evening, Paula called her into the living room, where Commander
Kyle, Aunt Vidala, and another woman named Aunt Gabbana
awaited her. Aunt Gabbana, who specialized in mediating marriage
proposals, physically examined Agnes. She declared her ready to
marry despite being only thirteen.

Agnes was removed from the Vidala School and spent her days
at home. On a footstool square she embroidered a skull that she
claimed was a *memento mori* but which she secretly considered a
symbol for Paula. Increasingly frustrated and bored, Agnes plucked
the Wife doll from her dollhouse and threw it across the room.
During her days locked in the house, Agnes began to wonder what
it took to become an Aunt and what kind of woman received the
calling required to pursue that path.

Aunt Gabbana came with a wardrobe team to design the special
clothing Agnes would wear in the period leading up to her wedding.
The dominant color of the new clothing was spring green, to signify
readiness for marriage.

Once Agnes had her new wardrobe, she was enrolled in Rubies
Premarital Preparatory, where young women from elite families
prepared for married life. Both Shunammite and Becka were in
her class. Whereas Shunammite was eager to marry, Becka was
extremely reluctant. Becka had begged her parents not to marry
her off. To Agnes, she also expressed her revulsion at the idea of a
man crawling on her. Remembering Becka's strong reaction to the
story of the concubine, Agnes suspected that Becka had experienced
sexual trauma.

Becka's mood deteriorated as the arrangements for her wedding
proceeded. One day, during a class on flower arranging, Becka
slashed her wrist with a pair of pruning shears. Agnes recalls the
ferocious look on Becka's face as she made the incision and then
said, "Goodbye, Agnes."

ANALYSIS: PARTS IX–X

Aunt Lydia's manuscript reaffirms the power she retains over Commander Judd. In Part V, Aunt Lydia stated that she came up with the Pearl Girls program at a time when Commander Judd's reputation had come under fire. He took credit for the idea, which saved his career. However, it was clear that Aunt Lydia's ingenuity gave her more lasting power than her male superior, who was reliant on her for ideas. In Part IX, Aunt Lydia again indicates the advantage she has over Commander Judd. In this case, however, her advantage lies not solely with her own ingenuity, but also with her greater access to information. Though Commander Judd summoned Aunt Lydia to update her on the latest news about Aunt Adrianna's death, Aunt Lydia already possessed the full story. In fact, she knew far more than Commander Judd, whose access to information remained limited to intelligence gathered by the Eyes. By contrast, Aunt Lydia had received a full debriefing from Aunt Sally herself, who told her in confidence that she'd killed Aunt Adrianna in self-defense. Aunt Sally also told her about the possible identification of Baby Nicole. Aunt Lydia skillfully hid this information from Commander Judd to retain her advantage.

Aunt Lydia's continuing account of her arrest and detainment foreshadows the painful decision she will make to join the ranks of Gilead's theocratic elite and gives context for some of her more heinous acts. During her first encounter with Commander Judd, she quickly realized that she possessed something of value to the new regime. However, lacking any clarity about what the Commander wanted from her, she invoked her legal training and refused to sign a "blank contract." What followed was a two-part technique of torture and pampering that served, respectively, to show the regime's power over her and to demonstrate the safety and comfort that could be hers if she agreed to cooperate. Commander Judd's two-part conversion tactic concluded with an ultimate test, the nature of which Aunt Lydia understood when she found the brown dressing-gown-like garment laid out for her in her hotel room. She knew instantly that Commander Judd wanted her to show her loyalty by participating in the public execution of other women. This also represents a symbolic choice between her own future, which could be assured through loyalty to the regime, and the humanity of other women. The choice set before her made Aunt Lydia feel trapped, and she felt powerless to do anything but put the gown on. Yet the

SUMMARY & ANALYSIS

reader already knows that she has since found ways to grow her power despite the constraints on her freedom.

The skull Agnes embroidered on a footstool square provides a symbol of her resistance to the accepted norms, as well as an example of her cunning ability to keep up appearances despite her resistance. To keep herself sane during the empty days she spent waiting for her family to marry her off, Agnes worked on her embroidery. Along with flower arranging and other domestic arts, embroidery represented an admirable activity for a future Wife. As such, her embroidery project made it appear as though Agnes accepted her new role without question. Furthermore, the image she embroidered had a long history in Christian iconography as a *memento mori*, which means "reminder of death." The choice of the skull therefore appeared to express Agnes's traditional faith. Yet in her mind, Agnes intended the skull not as a traditional *memento mori* but rather as a curse and a death wish for her stepmother. The skull also covertly expressed her growing concern that life as a Wife would be tantamount to death. Agnes's subversive *memento mori* demonstrates her continuing resistance to Gilead's norms under the cover of respectability. More broadly, it also introduces the motif of embroidery as a symbol of women's collective resistance.

Becka's suicide attempt at the end of Part X underscores how desperation can arise from oppressive situations. Agnes understood that Becka felt deeply averse to men and grieved over violence against women, hence her strong reaction to the story of the murdered concubine. Becka identified with the woman who ran away from her male master, and she couldn't stomach the injustice of the concubine's final, so-called sacrifice. Furthermore, just as the concubine suffered a horrific death, Becka concluded that her own marriage would be tantamount to death. Believing that she had no other viable way to escape her fate, Becka's sense of oppression gave way to an act of desperation. Her suicide attempt particularly affected Agnes. Like Becka, she'd grown increasingly suspect of Wifehood and of Gilead more generally. Thus, Agnes had compassion for Becka's experience. Becka's suicide attempt also foreshadows a future event in Part XIV when Agnes loses hope for her future and contemplates taking her own life.

Parts XI–XII

Summary: Part XI: Sackcloth

Aunt Lydia recounts a dream she had the previous night. She dreamt that she stood in the stadium wearing a brown dressing gown. She stood alongside other women in the same garb as well as several men. Each had a rifle, some with bullets and some without. They faced two rows of women. Aunt Lydia recognized the face of each woman, and she recognized former friends, clients, and colleagues. The women smiled enigmatically as Aunt Lydia and those beside her raised their guns and fired.

She returns to the point in her story when she put on the garment laid out for her in the hotel room. An hour later, men escorted her to Commander Judd. He asked her again if she would cooperate, and this time she said yes. Her agreement meant that she had to participate in a stadium execution, which she did. Anita was among the victims executed that day.

Aunt Lydia describes her first meeting with Aunts Elizabeth, Helena, and Vidala. Elizabeth and Helena had, like Aunt Lydia, been selected for their past professional experience. Elizabeth had worked as the executive assistant to an influential female senator, and Helena had served as a public relations representative for a lingerie company. Vidala, by contrast, had taken part in planning the coup, and she was poised to serve as the other women's spiritual advisor.

Commander Judd tasked these four women with creating laws and regulations to govern Gilead's women. Aunt Lydia insisted that if there was to be a separate female sphere, then women should have sovereign command over it. Commander Judd agreed, which boosted her confidence. In their early work together, Aunt Lydia observed the other Aunts' vanities and weaknesses. She believed she could rise to power by playing these women against each other. She lived by three commandments: "Listen carefully. Save all clues. Don't show fear." She committed herself so fully to the work that she almost believed the ideology she and her colleagues were making up.

Years later, Commander Judd apologized to Aunt Lydia for the extreme measures he had taken "to separate the wheat from the chaff." He assured her that her rifle had contained a blank.

This portion of Aunt Lydia's manuscript concludes with an account of a visit Aunt Vidala had paid her the previous evening. Vidala had come to report Aunt Elizabeth's concern that the food offerings left at the feet of Aunt Lydia's statue constituted cult worship. However, Aunt Vidala said she'd personally witnessed Aunt Elizabeth placing offerings herself, as if to create evidence that Aunt Lydia encouraged others to worship her.

SUMMARY: PART XII: CARPITZ

Daisy's account picks up just after Elijah told her about her real identity as Baby Nicole. Ada explained how they had worked hard to keep her identity safe. Even so, Ada worried that Gileadean spies might have infiltrated Mayday's ranks, meaning they had to take extra precautions.

Ada moved Daisy into another room in the same building. There she met Garth, who drove them to a new location. In the back of the van, Daisy asked Ada how she'd been smuggled out of Gilead. Ada explained that her mother had entrusted Daisy to her, and that she had traveled through woods and mountains with Daisy in a back-pack until they arrived in Canada. Daisy asked where her parents were, and Ada said their whereabouts were top secret.

The van arrived at a wholesale carpet outlet with a secret hideout area in the back. The news ran a story about Aunt Adrianna, the Pearl Girls missionary found dead in a condo. The police had ruled out suicide and now suspected foul play. Worried that Gileadean agents could attack soon, Daisy's caretakers brainstormed about where to move her. Elijah explained one possible plan. Mayday used to have a valuable source within Gilead who had corresponded with Neil via microdot. Before communications got cut off, their Gileadean source had promised to deliver a big document cache with seriously damaging information about Gilead's elite. In the event that The Clothes Hound was compromised, the source had proposed a fallback plan in which Mayday would send Baby Nicole into Gilead with Pearl Girls, disguised as a fresh convert.

Daisy expressed reservations but did not refuse the mission, and Garth taught her self-defense in preparation. Ada taught Daisy how to get along in Gilead's social environment. Daisy also received a forearm tattoo that, according to specifications dictated by the Gileadean source, featured the words "LOVE" and "GOD" arranged in a cross with both words sharing the "O."

Analysis: Parts XI–XII

Despite Commander Judd's pledge that her rifle had contained a blank, Aunt Lydia knows she's guilty of murder. When Aunt Lydia participated in one of the stadium executions, she and the other executioners didn't know whether their rifles contained a real bullet or a blank. The reader knows this in part because it is what happened in the dream Aunt Lydia recounts at the beginning of Part XI, and because when Commander Judd eventually apologized to Aunt Lydia for putting her through the traumatizing experience, he promised her that her rifle had contained a blank. Whether or not Commander Judd spoke the truth, Aunt Lydia recognizes that her guilt derives not from actually killing another human being but from her intention to do so. Traditionally, armies and militias have used the firing squad as a form of execution meant to exonerate the executioners from guilt. When many executioners shoot at a single victim, they cannot know whose bullet actually took that victim's life and hence needn't feel personally responsible. But Aunt Lydia understands that the executioners share a collective guilt because they were all involved in the murders. Because Aunt Lydia knows this, she cannot be manipulated by Commander Judd, who tries to inspire more loyalty in her by claiming to have spared her from firing an actual bullet.

As Aunt Lydia provides more details about her past, a clearer understanding develops of the ambivalence that has defined her life and continues to haunt her. The word "ambivalence" refers to a state of mixed feelings or contrary ideas that cannot be easily resolved. In Aunt Lydia's case, the ambivalence that defines her life stems from the fact that she has done terrible things, but with good intentions and in the midst of terrible oppression. As the dream that opens this part of the manuscript suggests, Aunt Lydia remains haunted by her participation in the stadium execution. Yet despite knowing how reprehensible her actions were, she finds little point in expressing regret. Instead, she focuses on the work she did with the other founding Aunts. If Aunt Lydia continues to take pride in this work, it's partly because it made her feel powerful. But her pride also stems from knowing that her power has enabled her to work against Gilead's interests in the long term. Aunt Lydia finds it impossible to judge whether or not her actions are defensible, and she remains haunted by the fact that her good intentions may not truly exonerate her.

SUMMARY & ANALYSIS

When Aunt Lydia admits that she occasionally found herself believing in the ideology she helped make up, she demonstrates just how susceptible human minds are to indoctrination. In the first weeks and months of their work together, Aunt Lydia and the other three founding Aunts labored to invent the laws that would govern women's lives. Creating such a complex set of regulations required a remarkable act of the imagination. Everything had to be invented, if not solely from the minds of the Aunts, then from a set of religious and cultural principles derived from the Christian Bible. Aunt Lydia immersed herself in this work, so much so that at times she forgot that the ideology was a product of her own invention. If a grounded and clear-headed woman like Aunt Lydia could fall prey to her own false ideology, then others of less robust intellectual ability must have had a much harder time seeing through the veil of indoctrination. This example gives a perspective on how so many everyday Gileadeans could come to accept their oppressive government. It also gives the reader renewed respect for Agnes and Becka, both of whom see through Gilead's lies, despite having been born and raised knowing no different way of life.

Part XII concludes with Daisy preparing to infiltrate Gilead even though she never explicitly agreed to take part in the mission, which calls into question whether or not the Mayday operatives are really as virtuous as their opposition to Gilead would make them appear. Although Daisy agreed with her caretakers that Gilead needed to collapse and hence acknowledged the importance of the mission, she takes care to note that she never properly gave consent. As both Daisy and Aunt Lydia have made clear in their testimonies, Gilead has worked hard to turn Baby Nicole into an icon for the purposes of propaganda. No longer strictly a human being, Baby Nicole now serves as a symbol meant to inspire feelings of national belonging and resentment of foreign nations in the people of Gilead. Daisy, who has studied the subject in school, understands Baby Nicole's role as an instrument of manipulation. Although the Mayday operatives are starkly opposed to Gilead's government, they seem equally willing to use Daisy—the real Baby Nicole—as an instrument for their own mission. They do not hesitate to send a teenager into a cruel and oppressive regime alone, highlighting the fact that people with extremely strong belief systems are willing to do risky, even cruel, things if it serves their political purposes. Though Gilead's leaders are ruthless in their oppression of women, Mayday's leaders also use a young woman solely to serve their own ends.

Parts XIII–XIV

Summary: Part XIII: Secateurs

Aunt Lydia describes how she installed a hidden camera at the base of her statue, hoping to capture footage of Aunt Elizabeth placing an offering. Several days went by without activity, but on the fourth day Aunt Vidala came at dawn and placed an egg, an orange, and a handkerchief embroidered with lilacs, Aunt Lydia's botanical symbol. Aunt Lydia filed the footage away for future use against Aunt Vidala and wondered how to use the information to turn her fellow Founders against each other.

Aunt Lydia turns to a matter that happened nine years prior to her writing, when Aunt Lise came to her office to report Becka's suicide attempt. Aunt Lise explained that Becka was threatening another attempt on her own life unless her wedding was called off. Aunt Lydia asked what stood at the root of Becka's aversion to marriage, and Aunt Lise admitted that the girl had a fear of penises. Aunt Lydia decided to admit Becka to Ardua Hall on a six-month trial, after which she could become a Supplicant to the order of the Aunts.

Wanting to know more about Becka's background, Aunt Lydia asked her if anything traumatic had happened to her involving a man, but the girl didn't wish to talk about her experience. Aunt Lydia declared that whoever it was, he would eventually receive punishment for his behavior.

Summary: Part XIV: Ardua Hall

> *I lay in bed that night with the three photographs of the eligible men floating in the darkness before my eyes. I pictured each one of them on top of me—for that is where they would be—trying to shove his loathsome appendage into my stone-cold body.*
>
> *Why was I thinking of my body as stone cold? I wondered. Then I saw: it would be stone cold because I would be dead.*
>
> (See quotations, p. 70)

Though worried about Becka, Agnes had no information about her friend's circumstances. Meanwhile, the preparations for her own wedding proceeded apace. Aunt Gabbana returned to present Agnes with three options for a future husband. One was the son of a low-ranking Commander, another was a young intellectual type whose previous Wife had ended up in a mental institution, and the third was Commander Judd. Though the adults presented Agnes with the semblance of a choice, she knew they'd force her to marry Commander Judd because of his elite status. That night, she lay in bed imagining herself stone cold and dead as each of the men tried to have sex with her.

Agnes had a week to choose her future husband, during which time she considered running away or committing suicide. One day, she overheard the Marthas talking about how Aunts sometimes drugged women on their wedding days. The official announcement of Agnes's engagement to Commander Judd came at the end of the week. The Commander came to the house to express his pleasure, and Agnes felt repulsed by his foul breath. She experienced a nightmare vision of "an enormous, opaque white blob" pursuing her with something like the mouth of a leech.

More Aunts came to make arrangements for the wedding and design the bride's dress. With only two weeks to go, Agnes's thoughts returned to suicide. She also imagined murdering Commander Judd on their wedding night, and she relished the thought of Paula discovering his bloody corpse.

One day, Aunt Lydia unexpectedly arrived at the house to visit Agnes while Paula was out. Aunt Lydia told her about Becka's enrollment as a Supplicant. She also implied that if Agnes herself had received a calling to become an Aunt, she might wish to consult her former teacher, Aunt Estée, about what to do.

Worried that Paula might drug her and lock her up, Agnes made a plan to contact Aunt Estée. She briefly visited the Aunt in charge of making her wedding dress to discuss design changes, then she asked her Guardian driver to take her to her old school. When he hesitated, she implied that her marriage to Commander Judd would make her more powerful than Paula and that she would later reward him for his help. He relented and chauffeured her to the school, where Agnes found Aunt Estée and expressed her desperation.

Aunt Estée agreed to intervene on Agnes's behalf and took her to a room in Ardua Hall, where Agnes saw a book for the first time. As she flipped through its pages, Becka entered the room and they shared a joyful reunion. Becka explained that her new name was Aunt Immortelle, and she described what Agnes would have to do to get through the mandatory six-month trial before she could enroll as a Supplicant.

Paula came to Ardua Hall to order Agnes to return home. During their meeting, Agnes followed Becka's advice and acted crazed. Aunt Lydia intervened and whispered something that caused Paula to relent. Afterward, Agnes passed her entrance interviews with the founding Aunts and received an official invitation to stay at Ardua Hall.

***

ANALYSIS: PARTS XIII–XIV

Agnes's two nightmare visions of sex demonstrate that, like Becka, she saw marriage as inevitably leading to powerlessness and sexual violence. In the first of her two visions, Agnes imagined her body cold and motionless as each of her three potential husbands crawled on top of her. Her sense of immobility suggests the imminent threat of rape. To make matters more disturbing, Agnes adds that in addition to being motionless, she imagined herself dead. In this sense, Agnes equates the performance of her sexual duties as a Wife not just with sexual violence but with her own spiritual or physical death. She sees marriage as the literal death of her self. Agnes's second vision came after she met her future husband, Commander Judd, for the first time. In this vision, Commander Judd transformed into a horrific larval creature with a leech-like mouth that threatened to suck her blood or drain her soul. This vision mirrors the first, in that it forecasts marriage as a nightmarish union that will sap Agnes of everything that keeps her alive.

Following Becka's attempt to take her own life at the end of Part X, suicide becomes a significant motif in *The Testaments*, particularly in this section of the novel. Like Becka, Agnes found it difficult to imagine what to do in the face of her inevitable marriage to a man who repulsed and threatened her. In her view, marriage would result in spiritual death, and if she tried to run away the Eyes would track her down, execute her, and string her corpse up on the Wall as a cautionary example to other women. Given the options, suicide appeared the most reasonable way to escape a far more terrible death. Agnes and Becka are not alone in their thinking. Suicidal ideation is extremely common amongst the women of Gilead. Shunammite, for instance, tells a gruesome story about a Handmaid who swallowed drain cleaner to escape her fate. Agnes also heard her Marthas lecture on the immorality of suicide, a lecture they would only feel the need to deliver if they suspected Agnes of pursuing that escape route. The fact that suicide is a rampant problem in Gilead shows how trapped many people—especially women—really feel.

Aunt Lydia's unexpected visit to Agnes constitutes the first time the reader sees Aunt Lydia taking direct action to set her plan in motion. It is also the first time the narrators meet and interact, though the novel has foreshadowed the eventual convergence of the narrators' stories. For instance, we know from previous sections that Aunt Lydia is actively engaged in tracking down the location of Baby Nicole—who is actually the novel's third narrator, Daisy. However, it comes as a surprise when Aunt Lydia shows up in Agnes's living room with no warning. Her unexpected visit indicates her desires to both undermine Commander Judd and bring Agnes under her control. As the reader already knows, Aunt Lydia has proof that Commander Judd poisoned his Wives. Now that Commander Judd has officially become engaged to Agnes, Aunt Lydia uses her knowledge to intervene and save Agnes's life. Yet Aunt Lydia would not necessarily have intervened solely to undermine Commander Judd. She previously stated that she fully understood the importance of waiting patiently until just the right moment to enact her plans. At this point in the narrative, however, it remains unclear what purpose Agnes will serve in Aunt Lydia's scheme.

Following Aunt Lydia's surprise visit, Agnes learned the power of acting. Before meeting Aunt Lydia, Agnes had felt hopeless and suicidal. However, after Aunt Lydia suggested that she might pretend to receive the call to become an Aunt, Agnes immediately jumped into action. Significantly, the action she took depended on carrying out a series of deceptions. First, she needed to deceive Paula into believing her urgent desire to alter her wedding dress design. Second, she needed to make her Guardian driver believe that her marriage would enable her to protect him from Paula's wrath. And third, she needed to convince Aunt Estée of the authenticity of her calling and the depth of her despair. She practiced her acting once again when Paula visited her at Ardua Hall. Taking Becka's advice, she simulated hysteria by dashing a teacup to the ground, which prompted Aunt Lydia to intervene and send Paula away for good. The success of this series of deceptions immediately changed the course of Agnes's life and provided her first taste of female power. She learns that, within Gilead's oppressive regime, women survive by being "prepared to wheedle, and lie, and go back on their word."

Parts XV–XVI

Summary: Part XV: Fox and Cat

Aunt Lydia discusses how much useful information she's gleaned over the years from the microphones secretly installed throughout Ardua Hall. She recalls how her finely tuned bugs allowed her to overhear when Becka finally opened up to Agnes about the foundational trauma that made her frightened of men. In bits and pieces, Becka told Agnes that her father, Dr. Grove, had routinely molested her. Aunt Lydia knew that many of Gilead's powerful men behaved horrifically and got away with it, but she decided that Dr. Grove's actions demanded retribution.

Aunt Lydia invited Aunt Elizabeth to tea. She asked her colleague whether she considered herself a fox or a cat. Aunt Lydia was referring to characters in *Aesop's Fables*. Whereas the fox had many tricks up its sleeves to get out of dangerous situations, the cat had only one: "When in extremis, I know how to climb a tree." In the story, the cat comes out with the upper hand. Not knowing how to answer, Aunt Elizabeth responded uncertainly: "Maybe a cat." Aunt Lydia accepted her answer and described Aunt Vidala's attempt to frame her for the statue offerings. Aunt Elizabeth expressed gratitude for the information about Aunt Vidala's treachery. In exchange for this information, Aunt Lydia asked Aunt Elizabeth if she would bear false witness about something.

Summary: Part XVI: Pearl Girls

Daisy, now going by the alias "Jade," dressed in ratty clothing and went with Garth into the city. They planned to live and sleep in the streets, where they would pretend to be in an abusive relationship in order to attract the attention of Pearl Girls missionaries. Garth instructed Daisy in how to act like a homeless person. She struggled to say things she didn't mean, but when the Pearl Girls showed her kindness and tried to persuade her to come with them, she shed real tears.

So as not to let Daisy appear too easily won over, Garth drove the Pearl Girls away. He and Daisy spent the next several days sleeping in various locations and eating fast food. On the fifth day, the Pearl Girls reappeared. Daisy pretended that Garth abused her, and the Pearl Girls made a deal to buy her away from him. He left without saying goodbye, and Daisy accompanied the missionaries back to their condo. There the Pearl Girls fed Daisy, allowed her to shower, and gave her fresh clothing. They explained how she would pose as a Pearl Girl to get out of Canada. It took a couple of days to prepare the necessary travel papers, then Daisy and one of the missionaries boarded a plane for Gilead.

After they landed, a group of men greeted them on the tarmac. Daisy's escort cautioned her not to look the men in the face. She focused on their uniforms, but she felt the men's gaze intensely. A car then drove the two women to Ardua Hall, where a ceremony was already underway in the chapel to celebrate the return of Pearl Girls and their "Pearls," or converts. Aunt Lydia stood on the pulpit and gave a welcome speech, then instructed the Pearl Girls to present the Pearls they had gathered. Daisy's Pearl Girl escorted her to the front, where Aunt Lydia placed a hand on her head and welcomed her.

ANALYSIS: PARTS XV–XVI

The shocking revelation of Becka's foundational trauma builds the sense of the corruption that persists below Gilead's apparently pious surface. Aunt Lydia describes how her vast network of surveillance equipment allowed her to listen in as Agnes coaxed Becka to explain what had turned her against men. Given the deeply traumatic nature of her experience, Becka was unable to tell her story in a single sitting, but eventually she revealed that her own father, the respectable dentist Dr. Grove, had sexually abused her since she was a very young child. Agnes herself experienced sexual abuse at Dr. Grove's hands when she went for an appointment in Part VI. Aunt Lydia knew that Dr. Grove had a reputation for molesting young girls. However, the revelation that he had turned his pedophilic predilections against his own daughter proved too much for her. Although she has witnessed significant male corruption over the years, she felt unwilling to let this crime go unpunished. Aunt Lydia here returns to her former role as a judge to pronounce a silent guilty verdict against Dr. Grove, merely one representative of the underlying corruption in Gilead.

Just as Agnes found a sense of agency in Part XIV by learning how to act, in Part XVI Daisy also learns the power of performance. From the outset, it was clear that Mayday's plan would only work if Daisy learned how to act. That is, she would only be able to survive her journey into and back out of Gilead if she could convincingly perform the role of a penitent and reformed convert. Yet when she and Garth first set out on their mission to get Daisy "converted" by a pair of Pearl Girls, she found it difficult to inhabit the role she'd been cast to play. On the streets, she felt like a fraud when she tried saying things Garth told her a homeless person might say. As such, she could not deliver a convincing performance. However, things changed for Daisy the first time she encountered the Pearl Girls. They spoke to her with what seemed like genuine kindness, and even though Daisy suspected them of acting, their performance truly moved her. Ironically, the Pearl Girls were the only people who seemed to see the humanity in Daisy, and after being used as a pawn by Mayday, she found something touching in their apparent concern. Daisy found a way to leverage this kernel of true feeling and turn it into a tearful performance that fully convinced her audience.

Upon her arrival in Gilead, Daisy immediately and intensely felt the power of patriarchal oppression. A group of men had assembled on the tarmac to greet her as she got off the plane. Daisy followed her escort's instruction not to look at the men, but she nevertheless felt their gaze on her. As she puts it in her testimony, she sensed "eyes, eyes, eyes," which felt like hands touching her body. Daisy's repetition of the word "eyes" recalls the name of Gilead's intelligence agency, the Eyes of God, as well as the traditional Gileadean blessing, "Under His Eye." Yet given her outsider perspective, Daisy experiences the gaze of male eyes not as a blessing but as a violation, the likes of which she had never felt before. In her testimony, she explains that the men's eyes threatened sexual aggression: "I'd never felt so much at risk in that way—not even under the bridge with Garth, and with strangers all around." In this way, Daisy's arrival in Gilead gave her first-hand experience of the Republic's male-dominant regime and confirmed her suspicion that Gileadean men actively oppressed women.

Parts XVII–XVIII

Summary: Part XVII: Perfect Teeth
Aunt Lydia writes that her greatest fear is that her efforts will fail, allowing Gilead to last for a thousand years. Despite her fear, she takes pleasure in the few "small mercies" available, such as the Particicution over which Aunt Elizabeth presided the previous day. Two men suffered the ritual participatory execution by a crowd of Handmaids: an Angel caught selling smuggled lemons and Dr. Grove.

Aunt Lydia recounts the performance that Aunt Elizabeth delivered in order to bring Dr. Grove to justice. She booked a dentist appointment, during which she ripped her clothing and screamed

that he had tried to rape her. At the trial, Dr. Grove vigorously pro-
tested his innocence, but his receptionist, who suspected his boss
of other wrongdoing, testified against him. Aunt Lydia watched
with Commander Judd as the Handmaids ripped Dr. Grove apart.
Commander Judd asked if Dr. Grove was really guilty. Aunt Lydia
replied that he was not guilty of assaulting an Aunt but of molesting
girls and so ruining them for marriage.

Aunt Lydia changed the subject to inform Commander Judd that
Baby Nicole had arrived in Gilead. She wanted to wait for the new-
comer to convert fully before informing her of her real identity or
presenting her publicly in Gilead.

SUMMARY: PART XVIII: READING ROOM

> *Once a story you've regarded as true has turned false,*
> *you begin suspecting all stories.*
> (See QUOTATIONS, p. 71)

SUMMARY & ANALYSIS

Agnes recalls when she and Becka first saw Daisy, whom they knew
as Jade, at the Thanks Giving ceremony for the returning Pearl Girls.
Agnes notes that Daisy's introduction to Gilead was harsh, since the
following day she had to attend the Particicution of Dr. Grove.

On that day, Agnes stood with Becka, who fainted at the sight
of her father's gruesome death. Becka felt responsible. Even though
she had told Agnes the story of her father's abuse in confidence,
Aunt Lydia must have found out somehow. Agnes registered that
this must be how Aunts gained their power: "by finding things out."

When Becka and Agnes returned to Ardua Hall after the
Particicution, Aunt Lydia brought Daisy to their rooms. Agnes
instinctively knew that the relatively placid life they'd led at Ardua
Hall was swiftly coming to its end.

Back when Agnes first arrived at Ardua Hall, Aunt Lydia had
allowed her to live with Becka, who helped Agnes choose her new
name: Aunt Victoria. Becka confided that none of the books she'd
read seemed as dangerous as she'd expected. Becka also told Agnes
that her acceptance to the Aunts wasn't a sure thing. She described
an event that had occurred just before she arrived, when an Aunt
named Lily had expressed a desire to live alone and work on a farm.
Aunt Vidala had submitted Aunt Lily to a severe punishment called
"Correction," and afterward Aunt Lily had drowned herself.

Agnes had spent the next six months learning to read and
write. At first she had struggled with the new skills, but Becka pro-

vided assistance. Agnes quickly learned that reading and writing didn't provide answers so much as lead to more questions. After six months, Agnes passed the entrance examination and officially became a Supplicant.

Though excited by her new status, certain events shook her certainty. One day, just as Agnes earned the right to read the Bible on her own, Becka warned her that the book didn't say what they had learned it said as schoolgirls. She told Agnes to read Judges 19–21, where Agnes found the story of the Concubine Cut into Twelve Pieces. Whereas the Aunts had taught that the concubine bravely accepted her sacrifice as penance for running away, Agnes saw now that their version was intentionally misleading. The realization inspired a crisis of faith in Agnes. Becka said she'd managed her own crisis by deciding that she could believe in Gilead or God, but not both.

One day three years later, when Agnes arrived at her desk in the Hildegard Library, she found a folder containing top-secret information about the death of Paula's first husband. The folder included evidence that Paula had killed her husband and framed the Handmaid. Paula had also been sleeping with Commander Kyle long before either of their spouses had died.

Over the next two years, Agnes received similar folders with dirt on Gilead's most powerful, including Commander Judd. Although Agnes didn't know who was feeding her the folders, she knew the knowledge they contained conferred power, and she longed to become a full Aunt.

ANALYSIS: PARTS XVII–XVIII

Aunt Lydia's strategy for sentencing Dr. Grove to death discloses the unconventional, roundabout tactics required to serve real justice in Gilead. Prior to the coup that established the new Republic, the United States' legal system had required a judge to carefully examine the available evidence in relation to the formal charges brought against a defendant. If the evidence did not prove the crime beyond a reasonable doubt, the judge had no cause to sentence the defendant. In Gilead, however, matters of law proved much more flexible, even slippery. Aunt Lydia understood that in Gilead, women had virtually no recourse against men's violence, particularly in cases of sexual harassment or assault. Officially, any sexual violence against women constituted a terrible crime. However, as Agnes and her classmates learned in the Vidala School, Gileadean society typically held women accountable for men's sexual temptation. As such, victims of sexual violence tended to remain silent. With no direct form of recourse available to charge Dr. Grove for molesting young girls, and especially his own daughter, Aunt Lydia took a roundabout path to justice. She fabricated a more obvious legal breach in order to convict him of crimes Gilead's law would never formally charge him with.

Becka's story of Aunt Lily's death adds to the motif of female suicide as a means of escape. The motif first became clear in Part X, at the end of which Becka attempted to kill herself with a pair of pruning shears, a symbol of female captivity. In Part XIV, Agnes began to consider suicide as a way to avoid marriage. She heard stories of other women who had killed themselves, including a Handmaid who drank drain cleaner, also a symbol of women's entrapment in the home. All of these instances of contemplated or attempted suicide have one thing in common: they arise from a sense of desperation in the face of oppression. With no options for pursuing liberty or happiness, many women in Gilead have chosen death. Aunt Lily offers yet another example. Her early studies as a Supplicant introduced her to information about other places and times in which women enjoyed more freedom. This information sparked a dream to live on her own and farm the land. Gilead's establishment considered any such vision of female independence dangerous, which is why Aunt Vidala subjected her to a violent "Correction." But this violence did not correct Aunt Lily's behavior. Instead, it taught her that Gilead would never allow women freedom, and she chose death over imprisonment.

As she prepared for the examination that would enable her formally to enroll as a Supplicant Aunt, Agnes learned the essential danger to the state posed by reading and writing. Upon first arriving at Ardua Hall, Agnes had assumed that the danger of writing lay in the content it expressed. This explains why she asked Becka if the books she'd read contained any dangerous material. Although Becka told her that the books with truly dangerous content remained strictly forbidden to Supplicants, Agnes slowly came to realize that the particular information conveyed in a book only accounted for part of its danger. Far more threatening was the way reading and writing encourage a person to think for themselves. More specifically, reading and writing enable a person not just to answer questions but to pose new ones. For example, Aunt Lily's death resulted in part because of her ability to ask new questions.

Her reading gave her access to knowledge about other ways of living, which caused her to ask what her own life would be like if she had an opportunity to exist under different circumstances. Such a question undermined Gilead's patriarchal authority, for which she needed to be "Corrected."

The deeper she went in her training to become an Aunt, the more tantalized Agnes felt by the prospect of wielding ever greater power. Agnes realized early on that the Aunts got their power by collecting other people's secrets. However, it wasn't until an anonymous source started feeding her top-secret information that she understood the kinds of secrets the Aunts really collected or how she might use them for her own personal gain. Everything changed for her when the first few folders provided her with dirt on two individuals she knew personally. One folder revealed that Paula had killed her own husband. Another showed that Commander Judd had murdered his previous wives, which implied that Agnes had avoided a death sentence by refusing to marry him. Armed with secrets pertaining to people who had personally wronged her, Agnes came to understand that an Aunt's power was neither general nor vague. Instead, this power was specific and pointed, and would enable her to take vengeance on those who had betrayed her.

Parts XIX–XX

Summary: Part XIX: Study

Aunt Lydia recounts how Aunt Vidala had startled her the previous evening by suddenly appearing at her private carrel in the library. Aunt Lydia had stuffed her manuscript away just in time. Aunt Vidala expressed her concern about the new arrival, Jade (Daisy's alias in Gilead). Vidala worried that the girl might be a Mayday infiltrator and insinuated that she'd like to interrogate her. Aunt Lydia said she preferred subtler methods.

Afterward, Aunt Lydia went to Commander Judd's home to speak with him. His new Wife, Shunammite, who had married the Commander after Agnes joined the Aunts, greeted her at the door. Aunt Lydia noted that Shunammite looked ill and offered to get her husband's permission to send her to a clinic for an evaluation.

Upon entering Commander Judd's office, Aunt Lydia noticed a nineteenth-century painting of a mostly naked young girl, hovering over a mushroom with a smirk on her face. On his shelves, she saw biographies of Napoleon and Stalin as well as rare illustrated editions of Dante's *Inferno* and Lewis Carroll's *Alice's Adventures in Wonderland.*

Aunt Lydia informed the Commander of Aunt Vidala's concerns about Daisy and concluded that her colleague was no longer reliable. She also suggested that he send Shunammite to the Calm and Balm Clinic for treatment, implying that she would take care of killing the young woman there so that he could "remain above suspicion."

To her reader, Aunt Lydia confesses that she feels "poised on the razor's edge," with two ways to proceed. Either she could continue with her plan to use Daisy to topple Gilead, or she could hand Daisy over to Commander Judd and rise to even greater power. She wonders whether, after having taken her plan so far, she could abandon her own desire for vengeance.

SUMMARY: PART XX: BLOODLINES

In Part XX, the witness testimonies of Agnes and Daisy begin to interweave.

Daisy explains her first impression of Gilead as a "slippery" place where she couldn't read people's facial expressions or understand the real meaning of what they said. She recalls how upset she felt by the execution she witnessed the day after she arrived. She wondered whether her mother, a Handmaid, had been as "feral" as the Handmaids who tore the two men apart.

The narrative shifts to Agnes's testimony, which recounts the challenges she and Becka faced in trying to teach Daisy how to behave in Gilead. Daisy lacked gratitude for the food she was served. She also spoke glibly about shaving her green hair, which caused a horrified Becka to cite Corinthians I: "A woman's hair is her glory."

In her testimony, Daisy registers that neither Agnes nor Becka approved of her. Yet she had no one else to speak to, and she suffered from fear and homesickness. She worried, too, that the person Ada and Garth had called "the source" might not even exist, meaning she might never get out of Gilead.

Agnes elaborates on other aspects of her disapproval of Daisy, who proved an untidy and unthoughtful roommate. More damning was the tattoo on Daisy's forearm. According to Daisy, it marked her conversion to the true faith, but Agnes notes how Daisy once called God "an imaginary friend." Agnes also recalls how Daisy performed strenuous exercises in her room in order to stay strong to fend off aggressive men.

Agnes continued to receive folders of top-secret information. One morning she found a file from the Bloodlines Genealogical Archives with information about her own lineage, including a photograph of her mother. The file also revealed that her mother had a second child: Baby Nicole. Agnes felt a mix of excitement and confusion.

One day, Aunt Lydia summoned Daisy to her office and revealed herself as the source who had been in contact with the Mayday operatives in Canada. She surgically inserted a microdot into the raised scar under the letter "O" in Daisy's tattoo.

Two days after reading the file about her mother, Agnes went with Becka to Aunt Lydia's office and found Daisy already there. Aunt Lydia explained that Daisy was Baby Nicole and that she was Agnes's sister. She also explained how, despite its noble goals, Gilead had turned rotten to the core, which both Agnes and Becka should understand, given the secret folders she'd been sneaking them for years.

Aunt Lydia then laid out a plan to smuggle Daisy out of Gilead. Agnes and Becka were scheduled to do their Pearl Girls missionary work soon, but Daisy would exchange places with Becka and go to Canada with Agnes in her stead.

Analysis: Parts XIX–XX

Shunammite's marriage to Commander Judd carries a tragic irony. As Agnes has explained, Shunammite was a bold and shameless social climber from an early age. When they were in the Vidala School together, Shunammite claimed to be Agnes's best friend. But Agnes understood that Shunammite only befriended her to gain access to power since Agnes's father, Commander Kyle, occupied a high position in Gilead's social hierarchy. Later on, when she reached marriageable age, Shunammite felt impatient for her wedding. She longed to possess the power and prestige that would come to her as the Wife of an elite male. Shunammite's commitment to achieving the most advantageous marriage possible eventually led her to abandon her first engagement. When she learned that Agnes had joined the Aunts, she took the opportunity to rearrange her betrothal and marry Commander Judd instead—all at Aunt Lydia's suggestion. And yet, considering everything the reader now knows about Commander Judd's propensity to poison his Wives, we see how Shunammite's great social achievement in marrying the man carries a tragic irony. All her social climbing has led her into a lion's den, likely to die a painful and pointless death.

Aunt Lydia's impromptu meeting with Commander Judd in his home office gave her a revealing glimpse of the man's character as an abuser. The first thing she noticed upon entering was a painting. He attempted to hide this painting from female eyes by placing it behind a door that, under normal circumstances, remained open whenever a woman was present. The painting reflected Commander Judd's perverse sexual attraction to very young women. It depicted a girl wearing little more than an inviting grin, suggestively hovering above a forest mushroom that resembled a penis. When Aunt Lydia concludes in her manuscript that the painting encapsulated the Commander's immoral desires, she implies that the phallic mushroom serves as a stand-in for the Commander and that he imagines himself about to have sex with the youthful nymph. The second thing Aunt Lydia noticed in Commander Judd's office were his books. In particular, she noted the biographies of two controversial male leaders: Napoleon Bonaparte and Joseph Stalin. Stalin, in particular, has a historical reputation as a man who enacted extraordinary violence in the service of his own political ideology. These biographies indicate that Commander Judd strives to attain a greatness, through war and conquest, similar to these men of the past.

At the conclusion of Part XIX, Aunt Lydia's confession that she feels poised on a razor's edge demonstrates her vulnerability. Despite the confidence she has exuded since she first became one of the four Founders of the Aunts and despite the power she has accumulated in the years since, Aunt Lydia remains doubtful about whether she'll be able to bring her plan to topple Gilead to completion. Significantly, her doubt does not stem from a question about her own abilities but from a desire to save her own skin. Like everyone else, Aunt Lydia is only human and hence may succumb to the temptation for even more power and influence, especially given the inevitability of her execution should she try to topple Gilead. A more skeptical reading is that Aunt Lydia is leveraging this climactic moment to add tension to her story. She has frequently shown concern about her future readers and what they might think of her. As such, the suggestion that she feels tempted to give up might be a ploy to make her look more vulnerable than she is and hence earn the readers' praise when she overcomes her own temptation. In either case, the fact remains that Aunt Lydia is taking a grave personal risk by engaging in acts against the state.

Part XX represents a significant turning point in the novel when the distinct narrative threads belonging to Agnes and Daisy begin to weave together. Prior to this point, the narrative followed a predictable pattern in which sections of testimony from Agnes and Daisy appeared on their own, separated by sections of Aunt Lydia's manuscript. Now, however, the narrative begins to alternate quickly between their distinct points of view. On the surface, this shift in narrative strategy reflects the fact that Agnes and Daisy have met and now live together at Ardua Hall. The oscillation between their points of view also serves the purpose of speeding up the narrative pace, accelerating toward the novel's climax. Yet the coming-together of their two testimonies also reflects that their lives are connected in more profound ways that have, until now, remained hidden. More specifically, the shift in narrative strategy draws attention to their shared origins and points toward their shared destiny. Agnes and Daisy are bound together by blood, and the journey they will take in ensuing chapters will bind them further through shared action toward a common goal.

Parts XXI–XXII

Summary: Part XXI: Fast and Thick

Aunt Lydia describes a series of troubling visits. First, Aunt Vidala came to protest sending Agnes and Becka on their Pearl Girls missionary work. She knew that Agnes had gotten unlawful access to her own Bloodlines file and worried that the knowledge about her mother would weaken her resistance to dangerous ideas.

Next came Aunt Helena, who also wanted to report that Agnes had been reading her own Bloodlines file. Aunt Lydia suggested that Aunt Vidala might have given Agnes the file, and before sending her away, she asked Aunt Helena to keep tabs on Aunt Vidala's movements.

Later, Aunt Elizabeth approached to inform Aunt Lydia that Eyes and Angels had raided Ardua Hall's print shop and confiscated the Pearl Girl brochures.

Aunt Lydia visited Commander Judd, who explained that someone in Ardua Hall had been communicating with Mayday operatives via microdots attached to the brochures. He raided the print shop, hoping to secure evidence. Aunt Lydia defended the innocence of the Aunt who worked in the print shop, but she mentioned her recent doubts about Aunt Vidala. With no concrete evidence from the raid and with other governmental officials questioning his effectiveness, Commander Judd suggested they should put Baby Nicole (i.e., Daisy) on public display and announce her betrothal to him.

Summary: Part XXII: Heartstopper

Aunt Lydia arrived at the apartment Agnes shared with Becka and Daisy to report the raid on the print shop and Commander Judd's plan to get engaged to Daisy on television. They revised their plan. Agnes and Daisy would leave first thing the next morning and follow a preset route to escape to Canada. To buy time, Daisy would write a note pretending that she had run away with a man. Meanwhile, Becka would hide herself so no one would suspect that Daisy had left with Agnes in her stead.

Aunt Lydia returned later that night with everything Agnes and Daisy would need for their journey. Agnes tried to persuade Becka to come with them, but Becka explained that they would certainly be caught if there were more than two Pearl Girls traveling together. Agnes and Becka expressed their love for one another. The next morning, Agnes and Daisy set off. They encountered Aunt Vidala just outside Ardua Hall, and Daisy punched her in the chest, using a heartstopper punch that she had learned in Mayday training. Aunt Vidala collapsed, and they dragged her unconscious body behind Aunt Lydia's statue. They worried that Aunt Vidala was dead, but they rushed into the car waiting to take them to a bus station at Portsmouth, New Hampshire.

From Portsmouth, they took a bus to a remote town, where they changed out of their Pearl Girl outfits and into jeans and long T-shirts. While getting dressed, fabric snagged painfully on the "O" of Daisy's tattoo. A man drove them to their next destination. Agnes thought about her early childhood and felt homesick for Zilla, Rosa, and Vera. In the middle of the night, the driver stopped and directed Agnes and Daisy toward a motorboat on a river. They got in the boat, which escorted them quietly toward a larger vessel, the *Nellie J. Banks*.

Analysis: Parts XXI–XXII

The urgent meetings Aunt Lydia has with each of her fellow Founders in Part XXI indicates a crisis moment in which everyone has begun to scheme against everyone else. Aunt Lydia has already played Aunt Elizabeth and Aunt Vidala against each other. When it became clear to her that Aunt Vidala was trying to frame her for traitorous activities, Aunt Lydia told Aunt Elizabeth about it, hoping that the news would sow distrust. Now she makes a similar move with Aunt Helena when she insinuates the Aunt Vidala may have furnished Agnes with the forbidden information about her lineage. Aunt Lydia has now mobilized both Aunt Elizabeth and Aunt Helena against Aunt Vidala, a strategy that shifts negative attention away from herself and stirs up doubt and suspicion amongst her fellow leaders. Aunt Lydia's targeted sabotage of her colleagues' trust actively builds toward a crisis moment, one that will, she hopes, provide suitable cover for the launch of her grand plan's final stage.

In an ironic twist, despite training to use her heartstopper punch on aggressive men, Daisy ended up using it to stop Aunt Vidala. Daisy first learned about this type of punch from Garth, the Mayday operative who trained her in self-defense back in Toronto. When she arrived in Ardua Hall, she continued her physical training in her room. Both events foreshadow her use of this punch at a crucial moment. After her exercise one night, Agnes and Becka insisted to Daisy that men were responsible for protecting women, but Daisy explained that it was the men who scared her. Significantly, Becka responded that if a man behaves aggressively toward a woman, then she must have done something to deserve it. Daisy rejected Becka's logic as a form of victim blaming. When Daisy made this claim, she implicitly underscored an important point: that women like Becka do violence to other women when they adopt patriarchal logic. In other words, Becka's belief that male aggression is the woman's fault is just as violent as the physical assault itself. It is precisely this kind of female complicity that Daisy defended against when she punched Aunt Vidala—a woman who actively helped men oppress women. Ironically, Daisy's training paid off, just not in the way she'd originally intended.

In contrast to Aunt Lydia's attempt to sow discord among her female colleagues and to Aunt Vidala's commitment to female oppression, a meaningful sisterhood developed among Agnes, Daisy, and Becka. As explained in Part XXII, Agnes and Daisy share the same mother and hence are related by blood. When Aunt Lydia revealed this information, they embraced each other as sisters. Importantly, they also embraced Becka as a sister, albeit not biologically related. Each of these three young women had troubled family ties. Agnes lost the only mother she'd known and felt discarded by Commander Kyle. Daisy learned that everything about her childhood had been a lie. Becka survived sexual assault at the hands of her own father and fled her family to join the Aunts. However, these women now gathered under the influence of Aunt Lydia, who had

become a surrogate mother figure for all three. By joining together
to carry out Aunt Lydia's plan, Agnes, Daisy, and Becka also formed
a deep bond of female kinship. This bond shines out in meaningful contrast to the many forms of violence that women perpetrate
against each other elsewhere in the novel and highlights the importance of women joining forces as the only meaningful way to fight
male oppression.

Parts XXIII–XXIV

Summary: Part XXIII: Wall
Aunt Lydia tells of how she visited Aunt Vidala in the Intensive Care
Unit. Another Aunt explained that the patient's recovery was uncer-
tain. As the nurse left, Aunt Lydia pocketed a small vial of morphine.

At lunchtime, Aunt Helena noted the absences of Agnes and
Becka. Aunt Lydia said she thought they were fasting before their
Pearl Girls trip. Aunt Helena then asked about Daisy's whereabouts,
and Aunt Lydia suggested she might be ill. Aunt Helena went to the
dormitory to check on Daisy and came back with a note in which
Daisy wrote that she'd eloped with a plumber. Aunt Lydia explained
that there had been a complaint about a lack of bathwater in one of
the dormitories and that Daisy must have met the plumber who had
been summoned to fix it.

Summary: Part XXIV: The *Nellie J. Banks*
Daisy recounts how she and Agnes boarded the *Nellie J. Banks*. The
captain explained their cover story: the ship was a cod-fishing vessel
that had just made a delivery to Gilead and now was heading back
to Canada. The captain directed the two fugitives toward a place to
sleep in the hold below deck, and he assured them that they'd be safe
there if the coast guard stopped the ship for an inspection.

Agnes and Daisy ate and slept. They awoke later in the night, as
large waves rocked the ship. Daisy, who felt sick and whose injured
tattoo had grown infected, complained to Agnes that God had
messed up her life. Agnes suggested that God may have messed it
up for a reason. Daisy realized that Agnes still thought the true goal
of their mission was to help save Gilead and purify it of corruption.
Daisy declared: "Burn it all down."

Agnes describes how worried she felt about Daisy, whose infected
arm had given her a fever. To make matters worse, the ship had engine
troubles. The powerful tide threatened to push the ship seriously off

course and possibly back toward Gilead, where the captain would be accused of woman-smuggling. Daisy's fever grew worse, and she asked Agnes whether she thought they'd ever meet their mother. Agnes said she did and that their mother would love them, but Daisy warned that sharing blood doesn't guarantee love. Agnes said a prayer for the two of them and for Aunt Lydia and Becka.

Later, the captain came down and told Agnes and Daisy they needed to offload. The ship was in Canadian waters but wouldn't be able to reach shore safely or take them to the Mayday rendez-vous point as planned. He instructed them to dress as warmly as possible and come to the main deck. The ship's crew lowered the fugitives in an inflatable boat, and the *Nellie J. Banks* moved off. Daisy steered the inflatable boat as the captain had instructed her, cutting across the waves at an angle and trying to avoid the tide that would carry them to Gilead, but soon the motor died. Daisy's infected arm had become useless. With only one arm, she instructed Agnes how to row with the emergency oars, and she insisted they'd survive if they just tried.

ANALYSIS: PARTS XXIII–XXIV

Aunt Lydia's act of pocketing the vial of morphine offers a moment of ambiguous foreshadowing. When she records the act in her man-uscript, she gives the reader a cryptic explanation of why she did it: "foresight being a cardinal virtue." In one sense, this fragmentary justification relates to Aunt Lydia's overall strategy throughout her years in Gilead. Ever since becoming an Aunt, she has collected all sorts of evidence and squirreled it away for some unknown future time when it might prove useful. "Foresight" thus refers to a gen-eral plan that involves having multiple contingencies in place. With this in mind, Aunt Lydia likely took the morphine not yet know-ing what she'd use it for. Yet the reader can hazard some guesses about how a vial of morphine might come in handy. Aunt Lydia knew how important it would be for Aunt Vidala to remain in her comatose state and thus be unable to reveal Agnes and Daisy's escape, suggesting that Aunt Lydia might use the morphine to kill her colleague in the near future. Aunt Lydia has also discussed her desire to control the circumstances of her own death, suggesting she might save the morphine for her suicide.

Despite committing to Aunt Lydia's plan, Daisy and Agnes remain in disagreement about the ultimate goal of their efforts. In Daisy's case, her goals have never wavered. She entered Gilead with the directive to find the source that leaked information to Mayday, then escape back to Canada with a document cache that would condemn Gilead. Furthermore, because she knew that Aunt Lydia was the Mayday source, Daisy understood that Aunt Lydia's true plan was to topple Gilead. Agnes, by contrast, remained convinced that Aunt Lydia did not intend to bring an end to Gilead altogether, but rather to root out those who had proved spiritually rotten and reform Gilead from within. Despite knowing firsthand how corrupt Gilead society is at all levels, Agnes continued to believe in targeted but ultimately partial change. By contrast, Daisy insisted on the need for change to be systemic. Gilead's spiritual rot had penetrated the foundations, and those foundations would need to be completely rebuilt. As Daisy put the matter: "Burn it all down." Aunt Lydia, as always, skillfully manipulates both young women to do her bidding, understanding that Daisy will desire the full fall of Gilead but that Agnes, who has lived her entire life in Gilead, will not be able to accept its complete demise as an end goal.

Despite being connected by blood, Agnes and Daisy's ideological differences lead them to understand that meaningful kinship relations require something more than genetics. This subject arose during a discussion about what their mother might be like and whether they thought she would love them. Agnes believed that it would be natural for their mother to love them. Daisy, however, cautioned against the belief that blood ties necessarily imply love. Both young women intuitively understood that love could exist just as well without blood ties. Agnes, for instance, grew up with an adoptive mother who truly loved her and whom she loved in return. Despite the grief she felt when she first learned that Tabitha wasn't her biological mother, Agnes soon realized that their relationship had real value. Daisy also grew up not knowing that her parents had adopted her, and though she had some reservations about their parenting tactics, she knew they loved her and wanted to protect her. Agnes also truly loved Becka and viewed her as a sister. Thus, both Agnes and Daisy understood that kinship was not strictly a matter of blood. Whatever might happen with their mother or even between the two of them, the success of these relationships would require real acts of camaraderie and love.

Parts XXV–XXVI

Summary: Part XXV: Wakeup

Aunt Lydia records the fallout from Agnes and Daisy's escape. Rumors have spread in Ardua Hall that Aunt Vidala's stroke resulted from an attack. Speculation has also arisen about the authenticity of Daisy's elopement note. Unlike the other major figures in Gilead's government, Commander Judd knew that Daisy was really Baby Nicole, and he summoned Aunt Lydia to his office in a fit of anxiety. Aunt Lydia secretly enjoyed his discomfort and made up excuses to buy more time. As she explains: "One is always buying something."

Meanwhile, the Works Department, which had investigated the water shortage in one of the dormitories, found Becka drowned in the rooftop water cistern. Other Aunts immediately condemned Becka, and many said they'd always thought the young woman was a fraud. Saddened by the loss, Aunt Lydia spoke at her funeral, hypothesizing that Becka must have slipped or fainted while trying to fix the faulty cistern.

Tensions continued to grow at Ardua Hall with new speculations about the two Pearl Girls who had reportedly left early that morning. Later, news came that Agnes and Daisy had been spotted at a bus station in Portsmouth, New Hampshire. Commander Judd reasoned that Daisy was a plant who had infiltrated Gilead under false pretenses, and he ordered a search operation. Aunt Lydia faked an apology to him for failing to see Daisy for who she really was. He warned that both their reputations—and their lives—were at stake. Aunt Lydia had a flashback to the moment in the stadium when she raised her gun and shot another woman. She asks herself, "A bullet, or no bullet?" She confirms, "A bullet."

Aunt Lydia visited Aunt Vidala. Aunt Elizabeth was there on duty and said that Aunt Vidala hadn't spoken yet. Aunt Lydia dismissed Aunt Elizabeth, and once her colleague left, she spoke loudly in the patient's ear, ordering her to wake up. Aunt Vidala responded instantly, telling Aunt Lydia she would hang for what she'd done.

Just as Aunt Lydia reached into her pocket to retrieve the vial of morphine, Aunt Elizabeth reentered the room to fetch her forgotten knitting. Aunt Lydia said Aunt Vidala had just spoken and that she had accused Aunt Elizabeth of hitting her and of being in league with Mayday. Frightened, Aunt Elizabeth denied the accusation. Aunt Lydia comforted Aunt Elizabeth, then got up to leave. On her way out, she implied that Aunt Elizabeth should smother Aunt Vidala with a pillow, making her death look like an asthmatic attack and protecting herself from Vidala's accusations. Aunt Lydia felt inwardly pleased to be taking care of both colleagues at once.

SUMMARY: PART XXVI: LANDFALL
Agnes and Daisy successfully rowed themselves to shore, where Ada and Garth were waiting for them. Exhausted from fever and intense effort, Daisy collapsed. A helicopter airlifted them to a medical center for refugees, where Daisy received life-saving antibiotics.

When Daisy woke up, Ada congratulated her on the success of her mission and said she was all over the news. The document cache concealed in her tattoo had revealed a huge number of explosive crimes that Canadian media had already started releasing to the world. Daisy wondered where Becka was and said that she had heard her voice on the beach. Daisy fell asleep again, and when she woke up, Agnes told her their mother was there. The three women embraced.

ANALYSIS: PARTS XXV–XXVI
Aunt Lydia's comment that a person "is always buying something" implies that social exchange operates in much the same way that economic exchange operates. In context, the meaning of her comment is relatively simple and straightforward. That is, Aunt Lydia knew that Agnes and Daisy needed as much time as possible in order to safely escape to Canada. For this reason, she needed to "buy" time from Commander Judd. Of course, no exchange of money occurs, so she's not literally buying time. Instead of financial capital, Aunt Lydia makes her metaphorical purchase with social capital, which refers to a form of wealth, or power, that arises from interpersonal relationships that have developed a shared sense of identity and values. In this sense, social capital's main form of currency is trust. Aunt Lydia has spent years developing her social capital in Gilead, manipulating others into believing that she shares their values. More than anyone else in Gilead, she has earned Commander Judd's trust. However, just as financial markets experience volatility, so too do social markets. Despite successfully buying time from the Commander, Aunt Lydia knows that her purchase will likely condemn both of them to death as Gilead collapses.

The scene in the recovery ward demonstrates Aunt Lydia's improvisational thinking process, which has kept her alive all these years. When she first entered the room, she intended to kill Aunt Vidala using the morphine she'd stolen from the hospital the last time she visited. However, when Aunt Elizabeth unexpectedly came back into the room, Aunt Lydia improvised. She quickly fashioned a lie designed to make Aunt Elizabeth see Aunt Vidala as a delusional and dangerous enemy. Leveraging this lie, she tried to manipulate Aunt Elizabeth into suffocating Aunt Vidala with a pillow. What Aunt Elizabeth didn't realize is that Aunt Lydia would film the murder and use the footage to condemn Aunt Elizabeth to death as well. Importantly, Aunt Lydia did not plan this particular series of manipulations but came up with it on the fly. This example shows once again that Aunt Lydia's revolutionary activities have not proceeded according to a single well-crafted plan. Instead, she has consistently practiced the art of keeping her options open, collecting evidence and ideas for when opportunity presents itself. Whereas the establishment of Gilead required a meticulously plotted effort led by men, a single woman's flexible thinking will take the regime down.

Part XXVI brings Agnes and Daisy's story to a hopeful conclusion with three distinct sources of optimism. The first relates to the successful completion of their mission. They persisted against all odds, including Daisy's infection as well as Gilead's systematic, state-fueled repression. The second source of optimism relates to the impact their mission seems likely to make. Even before Daisy had fully recovered from her infection, Canadian news programs had already begun to release some of the documents Agnes and Daisy had smuggled in. The revelations promised to spark international outrage and explosive conflict among Gilead's elite, all of which would lead the Republic to collapse. The third and final source of optimism relates to the joyful reunion between Agnes, Daisy, and their birth mother. Although in Part XXIV Daisy had cautioned her sister against assuming their relationship with their mother would necessarily be a good one, the novel concludes with the three women embracing, finally reunited outside of the patriarchal regime that had tried to separate them forever. Each of these women has made a significant contribution to female liberation, and their final gesture of love and solidarity expresses a revolutionary power.

Part XXVII and The Thirteenth Symposium

Summary: Part XXVII: Sendoff

In my end is my beginning, as someone once said.
Who was that? Mary, Queen of Scots, if history does
not lie. Her motto, with a phoenix rising from its
ashes, embroidered on a wall hanging. Such excellent
embroiderers, women are.

(See QUOTATIONS, p. 72)

Aunt Lydia speculates once again on who her future reader might be. She pictures a young woman scholar, bright and ambitious, who will labor tirelessly over her manuscript and eventually produce a "warts-and-all portrait" of her life.

She expresses regret that she won't live to see Gilead's downfall and explains her plan to use the vial of morphine to kill herself if and when the authorities come after her.

Aunt Lydia concludes her account by echoing a quotation from Mary, Queen of Scots: "In my end is my beginning." She imagines this motto embroidered on a wall hanging.

Summary: The Thirteenth Symposium

The novel's final section features the partial transcript of the proceedings of the Thirteenth Symposium of Gileadean Studies, which took place in June 2197 in Passamaquoddy, Maine.

Professor Maryanne Crescent Moon opens the proceedings by noting that Passamaquoddy, formerly known as Bangor, was once an important hub for refugees fleeing Gilead, as well as a key stop on the Underground Railroad in the United States's antebellum period. She then introduces the keynote speaker, Professor James Darcy Pieixoto.

Professor Pieixoto congratulates Professor Crescent Moon on her recent promotion to president of the association and apologizes for jokes of questionable taste he made at the previous symposium two years prior. Professor Pieixoto reminds the audience of the lecture he gave at the last symposium. A collection of tapes attributed to the Handmaid "Offred" had recently been discovered in a footlocker in Passamaquoddy, and he had presented his tentative conclusions about the tapes. Although some historians doubted the authenticity of the material and its dating, the professor declares that several independent studies have since confirmed his initial assumptions.

Professor Pieixoto goes on to describe two more recent discoveries. The first is a handwritten manuscript known as "The Ardua Hall Holograph," which had been concealed in a nineteenth-century copy of Cardinal Newman's *Apologia Pro Vita Sua*. Carbon dating places the manuscript in the Late Gileadean period. The manuscript was apparently composed by a certain "Aunt Lydia," whose name also appears in the footlocker tapes as well as several known Mayday debriefings. Professor Pieixoto reminds the audience of the need for skepticism and suggests the possibility that the manuscript could have been a forgery meant to frame Aunt Lydia. Nevertheless, he says much of the available evidence confirms Aunt Lydia as the manuscript's authentic author.

Among that evidence are two other recently discovered documents, which contain witness testimonies from two young women. These women learned that they were sisters and became involved in Aunt Lydia's plot to smuggle secret documents out of Gilead. Their successful mission led to the "Ba'al Purge," which thinned the ranks of the elite class and initiated Gilead's final collapse. A graduate student discovered the transcripts in a university library, tucked away in a file with a misleading title. She concluded that Mayday operatives must have transcribed the testimonies. Professor Pieixoto again cautions against taking the documents at face value, but he introduces a variety of evidence that strongly indicates their authenticity. He also speculates that the mother of the two women was the author of the "Handmaid's Tale" tapes.

Professor Pieixoto concludes his lecture by discussing an inscription found on an old statue of a young woman in a Pearl Girl dress. The inscription dedicates the statue to "Becka, Aunt Immortelle" and formally recognizes the "invaluable services provided by A. L." It states that the statue was erected by "her sisters Agnes and Nicole and their mother, their two fathers, their children and their grandchildren."

ANALYSIS: PART XXVII AND THE THIRTEENTH SYMPOSIUM

Aunt Lydia has labored to create an opening for women's liberation, and her vision of a female scholar discovering her manuscript represents a freer future that she hopes her work will help bring about. When Aunt Lydia envisions this female graduate student, she flouts the conventions that oppress women in Gilead. With the exception of Aunts, Gileadean law forbade women from reading or writing, and barred them from all access to information. This system sought to keep women ignorant and complacent with their lot and to prevent them from learning about alternative ways of living and thinking. By contrast, the graduate student Aunt Lydia imagines has not only received an education but has pursued her education to its furthest reaches. As a scholar, she doesn't just study the world; she actively contributes to the archive of human knowledge. In such a future where women occupy the highest echelons of learning, the basic rights that Aunt Lydia has worked so hard to revive will seem so commonplace that women might not even think much of them. As such, Aunt Lydia humorously suggests that her future scholar might even grow bored as she works on the manuscript.

Aunt Lydia concludes her manuscript by positioning herself in a lineage stretching back to Mary, Queen of Scots. Mary served as the Queen of Scotland from 1542 to 1567. Her reign ended in a moment of crisis that forced her to abdicate the throne to her one-year-old son. After trying and failing to retrieve the throne, Mary sought protection from her cousin, Queen Elizabeth I of England. But Elizabeth distrusted Mary and threw her in prison for eighteen years. History best remembers Mary for being convicted of plotting to assassinate Queen Elizabeth. Found guilty in 1586, Mary was executed the following year. In the period shortly preceding her death, Mary embroidered the words "In my end is my beginning." It is these words that Aunt Lydia invokes at the conclusion of her manuscript. By repeating this motto, Aunt Lydia draws attention to certain parallels between her life and Mary's. Like the Queen of Scots, Aunt Lydia was forcibly removed from power and unjustly imprisoned in oppressive circumstances. Aunt Lydia also sees a parallel between Mary's alleged involvement in a plot to take down Elizabeth and her own plot to take down Gilead. This quotation also reflects her hope that, like Mary, she will be remembered by generations to come.

Just as the book opened with a statue, so it concludes with one. *The Testaments* begins with Aunt Lydia describing a statue of her likeness that the Aunts had commissioned to celebrate her accomplishments. That statue portrayed a young Aunt Lydia presiding over two other figures: a Handmaid and a Pearl Girl. However, it remained unclear whether the sculpture's dominant figure empowered the other women or subjugated them. By contrast, the statue that concludes the novel clearly celebrates female empowerment. This statue depicts Becka, a young woman who readily gave her life to enable two other young women to complete a mission of the utmost importance. Furthermore, the statue also features text that clarifies in no uncertain terms who the sculpture is meant to celebrate. Commissioned by Agnes and Daisy, the statue celebrates Becka not only as a hero but as their sister. Like the first statue, this one also honors the work of Aunt Lydia, cryptically referenced as "A.L." Ironically, the statue of Becka honors Aunt Lydia's legacy more fully than did the earlier statue of her own likeness. Unlike the earlier statue, the later one truly encapsulates Aunt Lydia's belief in female liberation; the ambiguity of her purpose is gone, and now she is remembered as she wanted to be: a champion for female liberation.

IMPORTANT QUOTATIONS EXPLAINED

1. *I've become swollen with power, true, but also nebulous with it—formless, shape-shifting. I am everywhere and nowhere: even in the minds of the Commanders I cast an unsettling shadow. How can I regain myself? How to shrink back to my normal size, the size of an ordinary woman?*

These words from "The Ardua Hall Holograph" appear in Part III of the novel. In the first part of her manuscript, Aunt Lydia kept her identity a secret, but in this section she reveals herself as its author. Just prior to the quotation, Aunt Lydia addresses the reader directly and expresses concern that her identity will lead her audience to judge her based solely on her reputation. This worries her, because she knows her reputation is a formidable and not altogether positive one. She notes that she has achieved something of a legendary status in Gilead, at once "a model of moral perfection to be emulated" and "a bugaboo used by the Marthas to frighten small children." But Aunt Lydia also recognizes that anyone looking from outside will likely see her as a puppet of the patriarchal regime. It is to complicate such a judgment that she takes the time to compose her manuscript, which she frames as a defense of her life. Yet the power she has wielded may ultimately render her life indefensible.

In this quote, Aunt Lydia reflects on her complex relationship to power. She fully recognizes that she has become "swollen with power," which has endowed her with an intoxicating sensation of invincibility. But in spite of her legendary status in Gilead, Aunt Lydia cannot wield her power out in the open. Unlike Gilead's elite men, who possess ultimate control over social and political matters, Aunt Lydia must exercise her power underground, out of sight. This is what she means when she notes that her power has made her "nebulous—formless, shape-shifting." Yet it is precisely Aunt Lydia's capacity to remain invisible that makes her so formidable. Whereas male power appears in highly visible forms of violence, Aunt Lydia works silently, like a spy, relying heavily on surveillance and emotional manipulation. The relative invisibility of Aunt Lydia's exercise of power renders her a threat even to her male colleagues. Hence her claim: "in the minds of the Commanders I cast an unsettling shadow." Aunt Lydia clearly understands the power she possesses. She also clearly enjoys her power, which makes the idea of losing it and "shrink[ing] back to [her] normal size" difficult to stomach.

2.   *Did I weep? Yes: tears came out of my two visible eyes, my*
      moist weeping human eyes. But I had a third eye, in the
      middle of my forehead. I could feel it: it was cold, like a
      stone. It did not weep: it saw. And behind it someone was
      thinking: I will get you back for this. I don't care how long
      it takes or how much shit I have to eat in the meantime, but
      I will do it.

Aunt Lydia records these words in Part IX, as part of her account of her experience of the coup that established Gilead. Following her arrest, and after seven days of lockdown in a sports stadium, men came for Aunt Lydia and brought her before one of the men who led the coup: Commander Judd. The Commander invited Aunt Lydia to cooperate with the new regime, and when she declined, he sentenced her to several days of solitary confinement in the "Thank Tank." Doused in darkness and berated with sounds of violence against other women, Aunt Lydia grew psychologically disoriented. At some point, men entered her cell and subjected her to violent abuse. They came to her cell two more times, beating her and shocking her with a taser. Alone, hungry, in excruciating pain, and not knowing if or when her torments would end, Aunt Lydia broke down.

   In this quotation, Aunt Lydia confesses that her experience in the Thank Tank brought her to a low point. As someone who grew up in a poor, rural community with uneducated parents, Aunt Lydia had to fight her way into a better life. She demonstrated her grit by putting herself through law school, developing into a reputation as a skilled lawyer, and eventually becoming a judge. But the degradation she experienced in the first weeks after the coup profoundly threatened her spirit. Importantly, however, the violence that men perpetrated against her did not completely break her. Even though tears spilled from her "two visible eyes," Aunt Lydia maintains that she possessed a "third eye" gifted with an ability to see clearly through the crisis of the moment. This third eye, which symbolizes

Aunt Lydia's vast store of personal strength and fortitude, allowed her to discover a seed of resistance that remained hidden beneath the pain and horror she was experiencing. In this moment Aunt Lydia committed to nurturing this seed of resistance for as long as it took to get her revenge. The rest of her manuscript will narrate how her efforts came to bear fruit.

3.   *I lay in bed that night with the three photographs of the eligible men floating in the darkness before my eyes. I pictured each one of them on top of me—for that is where they would be—trying to shove his loathsome appendage into my stone-cold body.*

    Why was I thinking of my body as stone cold? I wondered. Then I saw: it would be stone cold because I would be dead.

QUOTATIONS

Agnes recounts this nightmare vision in Part XIV, immediately after Aunt Gabbana presents her with three options for her future husband. In Gilead, a young woman is conventionally understood as old enough to marry shortly after she reaches puberty. For young women of noble birth, like Agnes, the transition to married life begins with her transfer to a new school where she learns the skills necessary for a Wife to manage her new household. The young woman also dons a new wardrobe with spring green accents that visually signal her "freshness" and readiness for marriage. With these changes in place, Aunts initiate a search for potential husbands. And when the Aunts have narrowed down possible matches based on the men's interest and on genealogical research (to avoid accidental inbreeding), they present the options to the bride-to-be and her caregivers. The family has one week to make a decision, and though the final choice ostensibly belongs to the young woman, caregivers often force a choice that would selfishly benefit them.

The quotation above appears shortly after Agnes learns about the three potential husbands Aunt Gabbana has chosen for her. Agnes feels completely powerless following Aunt Gabbana's visit, partly because she finds all the men that were chosen for her revolting, and partly because she assumes Commander Kyle and Paula will force her to marry Commander Judd, the most powerful of the suitors. This sense of powerlessness leads Agnes to have a nightmare vision in which each of the three possible husbands takes a turn mounting her for sex. Her sense of immobility suggests the threat of rape and hence profound trauma. To make matters more disturbing, Agnes reflects that in addition to being motionless, she imagined herself as dead. Agnes therefore equates the performance of her sexual duties as a Wife not just with sexual violence, but with her own spiritual or physical death. In other words, she envisions marriage as a nightmarish union which will sap her of all strength and will. Agnes's decidedly dark vision of marriage reflects her growing sense that domestic life for women in Gilead is tantamount to death.

4.   *Once a story you've regarded as true has turned false, you begin suspecting all stories.*

In Part XVIII, Agnes recounts how an anonymous source within Ardua Hall began to slip folders into her pile of daily work tasks. These folders contained information that she, as a Supplicant Aunt, did not yet officially have the privilege to examine. The first time Agnes received one of these folders, she learned some top-secret information about her stepmother, Paula. Specifically, the documents revealed that Paula had been responsible for her first husband's death. Prior to his death she had already been engaged in an extramarital affair with Commander Kyle, and presumably she wanted her husband out of the way so she could marry her lover instead. To make this happen, Paula falsely befriended her Handmaid and pretended to help her escape from Gilead. After the Handmaid left, Paula murdered her husband and claimed that her Handmaid had done it. Authorities tracked the Handmaid down, interrogated her, and executed her. In the aftermath of the scandal, different stories about the murder circulated among the Marthas, but all these stories maintained Paula's innocence. Thus, when Agnes finally learned the real truth it had a shocking effect that made her distrustful of every other story she'd ever heard.

Agnes's distrust of stories also stemmed from another revelation that came when she earned the privilege to read the Bible on her own. The day the Aunts presented Agnes with her own Bible, Becka warned her that it didn't say what their instructors in the Vidala School had taught them. Agnes found out what Becka meant when she turned to Judges 19–21 and read the original version of the story she refers to as the Concubine Cut into Twelve Pieces. Back in school, Aunt Vidala had told a censored version of the story. This version emphasized the brutal violence perpetrated

QUOTATIONS

against a woman who ran away from her master, and it framed the violence as justified. With access to the original text, Agnes realized that Aunt Vidala had neglected to discuss how, even in the story, this violence was viewed as barbaric, and in fact led to a war among the twelve Tribes of Israel. In retrospect, Agnes understood that Aunt Vidala had intentionally modified her version of the story to inspire fear in her pupils. Now that Agnes understood this form of ideological manipulation, she would protect herself from it in the future.

5.   *In my end is my beginning, as someone once said. Who was that? Mary, Queen of Scots, if history does not lie. Her motto, with a phoenix rising from its ashes, embroidered on a wall hanging. Such excellent embroiderers, women are.*

In Part XXVII, Aunt Lydia concludes her manuscript by positioning herself in a lineage stretching back to Mary, Queen of Scots. Mary served as the Queen of Scotland from 1542 to 1567. Her reign ended in a moment of crisis that forced her to abdicate the throne to her one-year-old son. After trying and failing to retrieve the throne, Mary sought protection from her cousin, Queen Elizabeth I of England. But Elizabeth distrusted Mary and threw her in prison. In her eighteenth year of imprisonment, Mary became involved in the Babington Plot to assassinate Elizabeth. Shortly before her execution in 1586, Mary embroidered the following words: "In my end is my beginning." It is these words that Aunt Lydia invokes at the conclusion of her manuscript. By repeating this motto, Aunt Lydia draws attention to certain parallels between her life and Mary's. Like the Queen of Scots, Aunt Lydia was forcibly removed from power and unjustly imprisoned during the coup. Aunt Lydia also sees a parallel between Mary's plot to take down Elizabeth and her own plot to take down Gilead.

In addition to the motto that situates her in the same lineage as Mary, Queen of Scots, Aunt Lydia's reference to embroidery has important symbolic implications as well. Embroidery has come up elsewhere in the novel as a double-edged symbol, as when Agnes embroidered a skull on a footstool square in Part X. Embroidery represented a respected domestic craft every Wife should master. Agnes leveraged this fact to signal her virtue, and she claimed to use the skull as a traditional form of iconography known as the *memento mori*, or "reminder of death." Secretly, however, she understood the skull as a curse against Paula. In this example, embroidery represents a respectable domestic craft that nonetheless has the capacity for subversion. Like Agnes, Aunt Lydia considers herself something of an embroiderer, albeit in a more metaphorical sense. The art of embroidery consists of making many small stitches that, when carefully composed and skillfully executed, create an image. Aunt Lydia has "composed" her plot to take down Gilead from many small pieces of insight and acts of manipulation. These small units will, she hopes, come together to manifest her vision of a brighter future.

KEY FACTS

FULL TITLE
The Testaments

AUTHOR
Margaret Atwood

TYPE OF WORK
Novel

GENRE
Dystopian fiction; feminist political novel; spy thriller

LANGUAGE
English

TIME AND PLACE WRITTEN
Canada, late 2010s

DATE OF FIRST PUBLICATION
September 10, 2019

PUBLISHER
Nan A. Talese/Doubleday

NARRATOR
There are three narrators: Aunt Lydia, Agnes, and Daisy. Each narrator speaks from her own perspective using the first-person pronoun "I."

POINT OF VIEW
The Testaments unfolds through three points of view, each of which corresponds to one of the novel's three narrators, who speak in the first person. The first narrator, Aunt Lydia, provides a written account of her rise to power within Gilead and her involvement in the conspiracy to bring Gilead down. The other two narrators, Agnes and Daisy, each give spoken accounts of their involvement in the same conspiracy. The novel's final section, which takes place in the year 2197, features a historian discussing the written and spoken testimonies that comprise the rest of the book. This historian, Professor Pieixoto, indicates the possibility that one or more

of these testimonies could be false or misleading but concludes that they are probably honest accounts.

TONE

Dark yet hopeful. Like its predecessor, *The Handmaid's Tale*, this novel emphasizes the anxiety, oppression, and uncertainty that afflict women under the patriarchal regime of Gilead. Yet the novel's multi-pronged, female-led conspiracy to bring the oppressive theocracy down also indicates hope for life after Gilead's fall.

TENSE

All three narrators give accounts of their lives in the past tense. Aunt Lydia, who writes her testimony, sometimes reflects in the present tense on the current conditions of her life.

SETTING (TIME)

The not-too-distant future, about fifteen years after the events of *The Handmaid's Tale*

SETTING (PLACE)

Cambridge, Massachusetts; Toronto, Canada

PROTAGONISTS

Aunt Lydia, Agnes, and Daisy

MAJOR CONFLICT

The Republic of Gilead has subjugated all women. Aunt Lydia seeks revenge on all those who established Gilead and believed themselves powerful enough to control her. Agnes, who gradually learns the scandalous circumstances of her own birth and adoption, wants to reform the rotten parts of Gilead. Daisy, who also learns secrets about her birth, wants to help bring an end to the human-rights violations rampant in Gilead.

RISING ACTION

Each narrator recounts specific events and revelations that drove them to action. Aunt Lydia recounts how Commander Judd imprisoned her and then coerced her into becoming one of the four founding Aunts. Agnes recounts how she learned that she was the daughter of a Handmaid as well as of the horrific death of her father's Handmaid. These revelations led her to refuse her betrothal to Commander Judd and become an Aunt. Daisy recounts how, after the murder of her caretakers, she discovered her true identity as Baby Nicole, a famous child whose mother successfully smuggled her into Canada. Collaborating with an anonymous source in Gilead, Daisy entered Gilead disguised as a convert.

CLIMAX

Aunt Lydia identified herself to Daisy as the anonymous source and revealed top-secret information to Agnes and Becka about the rampant corruption in Gilead. Agnes and Daisy learned that they were sisters and embarked on a mission to carry secret information to Canada and to bring down Gilead.

FALLING ACTION

Aunt Lydia prepared for the fall of Gilead, encouraging the murder of Aunt Vidala and obtaining morphine to commit suicide. Becka was discovered drowned in a cistern, where she had hidden to buy time for Agnes and Becka. Agnes and Becka successfully arrived in Canada and were reunited with their biological mother. Historians convened many years later to discuss the fall of Gilead and the evidence of the main characters' involvement in its demise.

THEMES

Power; the collective nature of guilt; uncertainty

MOTIFS

Embroidery; escape; aphorisms

SYMBOLS

Agnes's dollhouse; Baby Nicole; the story of the concubine

FORESHADOWING

Foreshadowing in *The Testaments* mainly functions to heighten tension and anticipation. Each of the narrators recounts her story in the past tense, but each also frequently alludes to future events. Such allusions provide the reader with an obscure sense of what's to come, which adds to the tension of the narrative as it unfolds. As an example, Daisy learns from Garth how to throw a heartstopper punch, which she uses later to put Aunt Vidala in a coma.

STUDY QUESTIONS

1.   What is the significance of the novel's title?

The English word "testament" has multiple meanings, each of which resonates with some aspect of the novel. Firstly, "testament" can refer to a sign of a particular quality. For example, the novel opens and concludes with discussions of statues erected as testaments to notable qualities embodied by Aunt Lydia and Becka. This meaning of testament also relates closely to another word: "testify." To testify means to give evidence, and all three of the novel's narrators are telling their story—testifying—about their involvement in the plot that initiated Gilead's downfall. Importantly, the word "testament" only appears once in the novel, on the final page. After cautioning his audience against taking the testimonies of Aunt Lydia, Agnes, and Daisy at face value, Professor Pieixoto offers evidence for why he believes the testimonies are authentic. He discusses an inscription on a statue of a Pearl Girl that he believes Agnes and Daisy erected to honor their friend Becka. He declares: "I myself take this inscription to be a convincing testament to the authenticity of our two witness transcripts."

"Testament" has two additional meanings relevant to the novel. First, the word can refer to a person's legal will, in which someone declares what will happen to their property upon their death. Though not explicitly framed as a last will and testament, Aunt Lydia intends for her manuscript to be discovered and read following her death. Furthermore, just as death leads to the dissolution of the deceased person's estate, Aunt Lydia hopes her own death will be followed by the dissolution of Gilead itself. The third meaning of the word "testament" relates to the two main divisions of the Bible. Whereas the Old Testament contains the story of how a rift developed between humans and God, the New Testament reveals how God repaired that rift by returning to the world as Jesus Christ. Between the Old and the New Testaments, God undergoes a transformation from vengeful to forgiving. *The Testaments* projects a similar transformation of Gilead's society from something oppressive and patriarchal into something with the possibility of justice and equality.

2.   *What is the importance of Aunt Lydia's former career as a judge?*

Aunt Lydia's background as a judge indicates that she possesses a strong legal mind with the capacity to take in the big picture. This quality makes her a brilliant strategist and a formidable enemy. Soon after her initial arrest, men escorted Aunt Lydia to meet Commander Judd, a powerful founding member of the Sons of Jacob. When he asked her to cooperate with the new regime without explaining what cooperation would entail, she invoked her identity as a judge and told him she refused to sign a "blank contract." Insisting that Aunt Lydia was no longer a judge, Commander Judd subjected her to days of torture, the aim of which was to break her will and persuade her to rethink her position. Though Aunt Lydia eventually agreed to his proposition, she inwardly refused to abandon her training in law and justice. As she puts the matter in Part XI: "Once a judge, always a judge."

Under the new regime, Aunt Lydia immediately put her training as a lawyer and judge to work, carefully observing her colleagues and collecting evidence about any thoughts, behaviors, and actions that might come in handy at a later date. Aunt Lydia gradually expanded her capacity to acquire information by setting up a sophisticated surveillance network that allowed her to gather intelligence on all the Aunts living at Ardua Hall. Furthermore, as she gained more power in Gilead and found herself in the confidences of the regime's most elite figures, she collected damning information about the people who ran Gilead. Although Gileadean law rarely worked in women's favor, Aunt Lydia found unconventional ways to administer justice to those, like Dr. Grove, whose behavior she judged unforgivable. Finally, Aunt Lydia found a way to smuggle her collection of evidence out of Gilead and present it before the international court of public opinion, which would judge Gilead guilty.

3.   *In what ways is* The Testaments *hopeful, and in what ways is it not?*

The ending of *The Testaments* expresses hope because the novel concludes with Agnes and Daisy successfully completing their mission. They persisted through the emotional and physical difficulties that attended every leg of their journey. Their triumphant escape meant they could deliver the top-secret documents, which made an immediate splash as Canadian news media began to release them. Thus, at novel's end, the downfall of Gilead seems imminent. More optimism comes from the family dynamics between Agnes, Daisy, and their mother. Agnes and Daisy appear ready to work through their many differences and find solace in their sisterhood. In a novel that has shown how common it is for women to treat each other cruelly and thereby uphold the patriarchy, their willingness to find a common cause offers a hopeful message. Additionally, these young women are finally reunited with their mother, someone who also went through hell to escape Gilead and save one of her daughters. This reunion represents the happy culmination of many years of hardship.

Although the novel has an ultimately happy ending, a couple of details issue a warning. For instance, in a brief moment of dark humor, Aunt Lydia notes how history repeats itself. At the end of her account, she imagines that her future reader—a female graduate student—will occasionally grow bored of working on her manuscript. The graduate student will find it dull because it will be hard for her to fully understand or sympathize with the kind of oppression women faced in Gilead. Such a situation may seem positive, in the sense that equal rights for women would have become commonplace and familiar. Yet such a situation could also lead to the same complacency that allowed for the establishment of Gilead in the first place. Another cause for concern relates to the fact that the novel concludes with a male scholar, not a female as Aunt Lydia had hoped. Given that the novel braids together the voices of three historically significant women, it is significant that a male historian who has made sexist jokes has the last word—particularly given that history has traditionally been written by men.

How to Write Literary Analysis

The Literary Essay: A Step-by-Step Guide

When you read for pleasure, your only goal is enjoyment. You might find yourself reading to get caught up in an exciting story, to learn about an interesting time or place, or just to pass time. Maybe you're looking for inspiration, guidance, or a reflection of your own life. There are as many different, valid ways of reading a book as there are books in the world.

When you read a work of literature in an English class, however, you're being asked to read in a special way: you're being asked to perform *literary analysis*. To analyze something means to break it down into smaller parts and then examine how those parts work, both individually and together. Literary analysis involves examining all the parts of a novel, play, short story, or poem—elements such as character, setting, tone, and imagery—and thinking about how the author uses those elements to create certain effects.

A literary essay isn't a book review: you're not being asked whether or not you liked a book or whether you'd recommend it to another reader. A literary essay also isn't like the kind of book report you wrote when you were younger, when your teacher wanted you to summarize the book's action. A high school or college–level literary essay asks, "How does this piece of literature actually work?" "How does it do what it does?" and, "Why might the author have made the choices he or she did?"

The Seven Steps

No one is born knowing how to analyze literature; it's a skill and a process you can master. As you gain more practice with this kind of thinking and writing, you'll be able to craft a method that works best for you. But until then, here are seven basic steps to writing a well-constructed literary essay:

  1. *Ask questions*
  2. *Collect evidence*
  3. *Construct a thesis*

4. Develop and organize arguments
5. Write the introduction
6. Write the body paragraphs
7. Write the conclusion

1. ASK QUESTIONS

When you're assigned a literary essay in class, your teacher will often provide you with a list of writing prompts. Lucky you! Now all you have to do is choose one. Do yourself a favor and pick a topic that interests you. You'll have a much better (not to mention easier) time if you start off with something you enjoy thinking about. If you are asked to come up with a topic by yourself, though, you might start to feel a little panicked. Maybe you have too many ideas—or none at all. Don't worry. Take a deep breath and start by asking yourself these questions:

- **What struck you?** Did a particular image, line, or scene linger in your mind for a long time? If it fascinated you, chances are you can draw on it to write a fascinating essay.

- **What confused you?** Maybe you were surprised to see a character act in a certain way, or maybe you didn't understand why the book ended the way it did. Confusing moments in a work of literature are like a loose thread in a sweater: if you pull on it, you can unravel the entire thing. Ask yourself why the author chose to write about that character or scene the way he or she did, and you might tap into some important insights about the work as a whole.

- **Did you notice any patterns?** Is there a phrase that the main character uses constantly or an image that repeats throughout the book? If you can figure out how that pattern weaves through the work and what the significance of that pattern is, you've almost got your entire essay mapped out.

- **Did you notice any contradictions or ironies?** Great works of literature are complex; great literary essays recognize and explain those complexities. Maybe the title of the work seems to contradict its content (for example, the play *Happy Days* shows its two characters buried up to their waists in dirt). Maybe the main character acts one way around his or her family and a completely different way around his or her friends and associates. If you can find a way to explain a work's contradictory elements, you've got the seeds of a great essay.

At this point, you don't need to know exactly what you're going to say about your topic; you just need a place to begin your exploration. You can help direct your reading and brainstorming by formulating your topic as a *question*, which you'll then try to answer in your essay. The best questions invite critical debates and discussions, not just a rehashing of the summary. Remember, you're looking for something you can *prove or argue* based on evidence you find in the text. Finally, remember to keep the scope of your question in mind: is this a topic you can adequately address within the word or page limit you've been given? Conversely, is this a topic big enough to fill the required length?

GOOD QUESTIONS

"Are Romeo and Juliet's parents responsible for the deaths of their children?"

"Why do pigs keep showing up in Lord of the Flies?"

"Are Dr. Frankenstein and his monster alike? How?"

BAD QUESTIONS

"What happens to Scout in To Kill a Mockingbird?"

"What do the other characters in Julius Caesar *think about Caesar?"*

"How does Hester Prynne in The Scarlet Letter *remind me of my sister?"*

---

2. COLLECT EVIDENCE

Once you know what question you want to answer, it's time to scour the book for things that will help you answer the question. Don't worry if you don't know what you want to say yet—right now you're just collecting ideas and material and letting it all percolate. Keep track of passages, symbols, images, or scenes that deal with your topic. Eventually, you'll start making connections between these examples, and your thesis will emerge.

Here's a brief summary of the various parts that compose each and every work of literature. These are the elements that you will analyze in your essay and that you will offer as evidence to support your arguments. For more on the parts of literary works, see the Glossary of Literary Terms at the end of this section.

Elements of Story   These are the *what*s of the work—what happens, where it happens, and to whom it happens.

- **Plot:** All the events and actions of the work.

- **Character:** The people who act and are acted on in a literary work. The main character of a work is known as the *protagonist.*

- **Conflict:** The central tension in the work. In most cases, the protagonist wants something, while opposing forces (antagonists) hinder the protagonist's progress.

- **Setting:** When and where the work takes place. Elements of setting include location, time period, time of day, weather, social atmosphere, and economic conditions.

- **Narrator:** The person telling the story. The narrator may straightforwardly report what happens, convey the subjective opinions and perceptions of one or more characters, or provide commentary and opinion in his or her own voice.

- **Themes:** The main idea or message of the work—usually an abstract idea about people, society, or life in general. A work may have many themes, which may be in tension with one another.

Elements of Style   These are the *how*s—how the characters speak, how the story is constructed, and how language is used throughout the work.

- **Structure and organization:** How the parts of the work are assembled. Some novels are narrated in a linear, chronological fashion, while others skip around in time. Some plays follow a traditional three- or five-act structure, while others are a series of loosely connected scenes. Some authors deliberately leave gaps in their work, leaving readers to puzzle out the missing information. A work's structure and organization can tell you a lot about the kind of message it wants to convey.

- **Point of view:** The perspective from which a story is told. In *first-person point of view*, the narrator involves himself or herself in the story. ("I went to the store"; "We watched in horror as the bird slammed into the window.") A first-person narrator is usually the protagonist of the work, but not always. In *third-person point of view*, the narrator does not participate

LITERARY ANALYSIS

in the story. A third-person narrator may closely follow a specific character, recounting that individual character's thoughts or experiences, or it may be what we call an *omniscient* narrator. Omniscient narrators see and know all: they can witness any event in any time or place and are privy to the inner thoughts and feelings of all characters. Remember that the narrator and the author are not the same thing!

- **Diction:** Word choice. Whether a character uses dry, clinical language or flowery prose with lots of exclamation points can tell you a lot about his or her attitude and personality.

- **Syntax:** Word order and sentence construction. Syntax is a crucial part of establishing an author's narrative voice. Ernest Hemingway, for example, is known for writing in very short, straightforward sentences, while James Joyce characteristically wrote in long, extremely complicated lines.

- **Tone:** The mood or feeling of the text. Diction and syntax often contribute to the tone of a work. A novel written in short, clipped sentences that use small, simple words might feel brusque, cold, or matter-of-fact.

- **Imagery:** Language that appeals to the senses, representing things that can be seen, smelled, heard, tasted, or touched.

- **Figurative language:** Language that is not meant to be interpreted literally. The most common types of figurative language are *metaphors* and *similes*, which compare two unlike things in order to suggest a similarity between them—for example, "All the world's a stage," or "The moon is like a ball of green cheese." (Metaphors say one thing *is* another thing; similes claim that one thing is *like* another thing.)

3. CONSTRUCT A THESIS

When you've examined all the evidence you've collected and know how you want to answer the question, it's time to write your thesis statement. A *thesis* is a claim about a work of literature that needs to be supported by evidence and arguments. The thesis statement is the heart of the literary essay, and the bulk of your paper will be spent trying to prove this claim. A good thesis will be:

- **Arguable.** "*The Great Gatsby* describes New York society in the 1920s" isn't a thesis—it's a fact.

- **Provable through textual evidence.** "*Hamlet* is a confusing but ultimately very well-written play" is a weak thesis because it offers the writer's personal opinion about the book. Yes, it's arguable, but it's not a claim that can be proved or supported with examples taken from the play itself.

- **Surprising.** "Both George and Lenny change a great deal in *Of Mice and Men*" is a weak thesis because it's obvious. A really strong thesis will argue for a reading of the text that is not immediately apparent.

- **Specific.** "Dr. Frankenstein's monster tells us a lot about the human condition" is *almost* a really great thesis statement, but it's still too vague. What does the writer mean by "a lot"? *How* does the monster tell us so much about the human condition?

GOOD THESIS STATEMENTS

Question: In *Romeo and Juliet*, which is more powerful in shaping the lovers' story: fate or foolishness?

Thesis: "Though Shakespeare defines Romeo and Juliet as 'star-crossed lovers,' and images of stars and planets appear throughout the play, a closer examination of that celestial imagery reveals that the stars are merely witnesses to the characters' foolish activities and not the causes themselves."

Question: How does the bell jar function as a symbol in Sylvia Plath's *The Bell Jar*?

Thesis: "A bell jar is a bell-shaped glass that has three basic uses: to hold a specimen for observation, to contain gases, and to maintain a vacuum. The bell jar appears in each of these capacities in *The Bell Jar*, Plath's semi-autobiographical novel, and each appearance marks a different stage in Esther's mental breakdown."

Question: Would Piggy in *The Lord of the Flies* make a good island leader if he were given the chance?

Thesis: "Though the intelligent, rational, and innovative Piggy has the mental characteristics of a good leader, he ultimately lacks the social skills necessary to be an effective one. Golding emphasizes this point by giving Piggy a foil in the charismatic Jack, whose magnetic personality allows him to capture and wield power effectively, if not always wisely."

4. DEVELOP AND ORGANIZE ARGUMENTS

The reasons and examples that support your thesis will form the middle paragraphs of your essay. Since you can't really write your thesis statement until you know how you'll structure your argument, you'll probably end up working on steps 3 and 4 at the same time. There's no single method of argumentation that will work in every context. One essay prompt might ask you to compare and contrast two characters, while another asks you to trace an image through a given work of literature. These questions require different kinds of answers and therefore different kinds of arguments. Below, we'll discuss three common kinds of essay prompts and some strategies for constructing a solid, well-argued case.

TYPES OF LITERARY ESSAYS

- **Compare and contrast**

  Compare and contrast the characters of Huck and Jim in The Adventures of Huckleberry Finn.

  Chances are you've written this kind of essay before. In an academic literary context, you'll organize your arguments the same way you would in any other class. You can either go *subject by subject* or *point by point*. In the former, you'll discuss one character first and then the second. In the latter, you'll choose several traits (attitude toward life, social status, images and metaphors associated with the character) and devote a paragraph to each. You may want to use a mix of these two approaches—for example, you may want to spend a paragraph apiece broadly sketching Huck's and Jim's personalities before transitioning to a paragraph or two describing a few key points of comparison. This can be a highly effective strategy if you want to make a counterintuitive argument—that, despite seeming to be totally different, the two characters or objects being compared are actually similar in a very important way (or vice versa). Remember that your essay should reveal something fresh or unexpected about the text, so think beyond the obvious parallels and differences.

- **Trace**

  Choose an image—for example, birds, knives, or eyes—and trace that image throughout Macbeth.

  Sounds pretty easy, right? All you need to do is read the play, underline every appearance of a knife in *Macbeth* and then list them in your essay in the order they appear, right? Well, not exactly. Your teacher doesn't want a simple catalog of examples. He or she wants to see you make *connections* between those examples—that's the difference between summarizing and analyzing. In the *Macbeth* example, think about the different contexts in which knives appear in the play and to what effect. In *Macbeth*, there are real knives and imagined knives; knives that kill and knives that simply threaten. Categorize and classify your examples to give them some order. Finally, always keep the overall effect in mind. After you choose and analyze your examples, you should come to some greater understanding about the work, as well as the role of your chosen image, symbol, or phrase in developing the major themes and stylistic strategies of that work.

- **Debate**

  Is the society depicted in 1984 *good for its citizens?*

  In this kind of essay, you're being asked to debate a moral, ethical, or aesthetic issue regarding the work. You might be asked to judge a character or group of characters *(Is Caesar responsible for his own demise?)* or the work itself *(Is Jane Eyre a feminist novel?)*. For this kind of essay, there are two important points to keep in mind. First, don't simply base your arguments on your personal feelings and reactions. Every literary essay expects you to read and analyze the work, so search for evidence in the text. What do characters in *1984* have to say about the government of Oceania? What images does Orwell use that might give you a hint about his attitude toward the government? As in any debate, you also need to make sure that you define all the necessary terms before you begin to argue your case. What does it mean to be a "good" society? What makes a novel "feminist"? You should define your terms right up front, in the first paragraph after your introduction.

Second, remember that strong literary essays make contrary and surprising arguments. Try to think outside the box. In the *1984* example above, it seems like the obvious answer would be no, the totalitarian society depicted in Orwell's novel is *not* good for its citizens. But can you think of any arguments for the opposite side? Even if your final assertion is that the novel depicts a cruel, repressive, and therefore harmful society, acknowledging and responding to the counterargument will strengthen your overall case.

5. WRITE THE INTRODUCTION

Your introduction sets up the entire essay. It's where you present your topic and articulate the particular issues and questions you'll be addressing. It's also where you, as the writer, introduce yourself to your readers. A persuasive literary essay immediately establishes its writer as a knowledgeable, authoritative figure.

An introduction can vary in length depending on the overall length of the essay, but in a traditional five-paragraph essay it should be no longer than one paragraph. However long it is, your introduction needs to:

- **Provide any necessary context.** Your introduction should situate the reader and let him or her know what to expect. What book are you discussing? Which characters? What topic will you be addressing?

- **Answer the "So what?" question.** Why is this topic important, and why is your particular position on the topic noteworthy? Ideally, your introduction should pique the reader's interest by suggesting how your argument is surprising or otherwise counterintuitive. Literary essays make unexpected connections and reveal less-than-obvious truths.

- **Present your thesis.** This usually happens at or very near the end of your introduction.

- **Indicate the shape of the essay to come.** Your reader should finish reading your introduction with a good sense of the scope of your essay as well as the path you'll take toward proving your thesis. You don't need to spell out every step, but you do need to suggest the organizational pattern you'll be using.

Your introduction should not:

- **Be vague.** Beware of the two killer words in literary analysis: *interesting* and *important.* Of course, the work, question, or example is interesting and important—that's why you're writing about it!

- **Open with any grandiose assertions.** Many student readers think that beginning their essays with a flamboyant statement, such as "Since the dawn of time, writers have been fascinated by the topic of free will," makes them sound important and commanding. In fact, it sounds pretty amateurish.

- **Wildly praise the work.** Another typical mistake student writers make is extolling the work or author. Your teacher doesn't need to be told that "Shakespeare is perhaps the greatest writer in the English language." You can mention a work's reputation in passing—by referring to *The Adventures of Huckleberry Finn* as "Mark Twain's enduring classic," for example—but don't make a point of bringing it up unless that reputation is key to your argument.

- **Go off-topic.** Keep your introduction streamlined and to the point. Don't feel the need to throw in all kinds of bells and whistles in order to impress your reader—just get to the point as quickly as you can, without skimping on any of the required steps.

6. Write the Body Paragraphs

Once you've written your introduction, you'll take the arguments you developed in step 4 and turn them into your body paragraphs. The organization of this middle section of your essay will largely be determined by the argumentative strategy you use, but no matter how you arrange your thoughts, your body paragraphs need to do the following:

- **Begin with a strong topic sentence.** Topic sentences are like signs on a highway: they tell the readers where they are and where they're going. A good topic sentence not only alerts readers to what issue will be discussed in the following paragraphs but also gives them a sense of what argument will be made *about* that issue. "Rumor and gossip play an important role in *The Crucible*" isn't a strong topic sentence because it doesn't tell us very much. "The community's constant gossiping creates an environment that allows false accusations to flourish" is a much stronger topic sentence—

it not only tells us what the paragraph will discuss (gossip) but how the paragraph will discuss the topic (by showing how gossip creates a set of conditions that leads to the play's climactic action).

- **Fully and completely develop a single thought.** Don't skip around in your paragraph or try to stuff in too much material. Body paragraphs are like bricks: each individual one needs to be strong and sturdy or the entire structure will collapse. Make sure you have really proven your point before moving on to the next one.

- **Use transitions effectively.** Good literary essay writers know that each paragraph must be clearly and strongly linked to the material around it. Think of each paragraph as a response to the one that precedes it. Use transition words and phrases such as *however*, *similarly*, *on the contrary*, *therefore*, and *furthermore* to indicate what kind of response you're making.

---

7. WRITE THE CONCLUSION

Just as you used the introduction to ground your readers in the topic before providing your thesis, you'll use the conclusion to quickly summarize the specifics learned thus far and then hint at the broader implications of your topic. A good conclusion will:

- **Do more than simply restate the thesis.** If your thesis argued that *The Catcher in the Rye* can be read as a Christian allegory, don't simply end your essay by saying, "And that is why *The Catcher in the Rye* can be read as a Christian allegory." If you've constructed your arguments well, this kind of statement will just be redundant.

- **Synthesize the arguments rather than summarizing them.** Similarly, don't repeat the details of your body paragraphs in your conclusion. The readers have already read your essay, and chances are it's not so long that they've forgotten all your points by now.

- **Revisit the "So what?" question.** In your introduction, you made a case for why your topic and position are important. You should close your essay with the same sort of gesture. What do your readers know now that they didn't know before? How will that knowledge help them better appreciate or understand the work overall?

- **Move from the specific to the general.** Your essay has most likely treated a very specific element of the work—a single character, a small set of images, or a particular passage. In your conclusion, try to show how this narrow discussion has wider implications for the work overall. If your essay on *To Kill a Mockingbird* focused on the character of Boo Radley, for example, you might want to include a bit in the conclusion about how he fits into the novel's larger message about childhood, innocence, or family life.

- **Stay relevant.** Your conclusion should suggest new directions of thought, but it shouldn't be treated as an opportunity to pad your essay with all the extra, interesting ideas you came up with during your brainstorming sessions but couldn't fit into the essay proper. Don't attempt to stuff in unrelated queries or too many abstract thoughts.

- **Avoid making overblown closing statements.** A conclusion should open up your highly specific, focused discussion, but it should do so without drawing a sweeping lesson about life or human nature. Making such observations may be part of the point of reading, but it's almost always a mistake in essays, where these observations tend to sound overly dramatic or simply silly.

A+ Essay Checklist

Congratulations! If you've followed all the steps we've outlined, you should have a solid literary essay to show for all your efforts. What if you've got your sights set on an A+? To write the kind of superlative essay that will be rewarded with a perfect grade, keep the following rubric in mind. These are the qualities that teachers expect to see in a truly A+ essay. How does yours stack up?

- ✓ Demonstrates a thorough understanding of the book
- ✓ Presents an original, compelling argument
- ✓ Thoughtfully analyzes the text's formal elements
- ✓ Uses appropriate and insightful examples
- ✓ Structures ideas in a logical and progressive order
- ✓ Demonstrates a mastery of sentence construction, transitions, grammar, spelling, and word choice

LITERARY ANALYSIS

SUGGESTED ESSAY TOPICS

1. What makes Baby Nicole such an important symbol inside and outside of Gilead?

2. What significance does Aunt Lydia's retelling of Aesop's story of the Fox and the Cat have in the novel?

3. Why does Becka insist that a person can believe in God or in Gilead, but not both?

4. Describe and analyze the relationship between Aunt Lydia and her fellow Aunts.

5. Why do many of the characters have multiple names, and what is the significance of this multiplicity?

6. What do Agnes and Daisy have in common, and how are they fundamentally different?

7. What does it mean that the novel ends with a lecture delivered by a male historian?

GLOSSARY OF LITERARY TERMS

ANTAGONIST

The entity that acts to frustrate the goals of the *protagonist*. The antagonist is usually another *character* but may also be a nonhuman force.

ANTIHERO / ANTIHEROINE

A *protagonist* who is not admirable or who challenges notions of what should be considered admirable.

CHARACTER

A person, animal, or any other thing with a personality that appears in a *narrative*.

CLIMAX

The moment of greatest intensity in a text or the major turning point in the *plot*.

CONFLICT

The central struggle that moves the *plot* forward. The conflict can be the *protagonist*'s struggle against fate, nature, society, or another person.

FIRST-PERSON POINT OF VIEW

A literary style in which the *narrator* tells the story from his or her own *point of view* and refers to himself or herself as "I." The narrator may be an active participant in the story or just an observer.

HERO / HEROINE

The principal *character* in a literary work or *narrative*.

IMAGERY

Language that brings to mind sense-impressions, representing things that can be seen, smelled, heard, tasted, or touched.

MOTIF

A recurring idea, structure, contrast, or device that develops or informs the major *themes* of a work of literature.

NARRATIVE

A story.

NARRATOR

The person (sometimes a *character*) who tells a story; the *voice* assumed by the writer. The narrator and the author of the work of literature are not the same thing.

PLOT

The arrangement of the events in a story, including the sequence in which they are told, the relative emphasis they are given, and the causal connections between events.

POINT OF VIEW

The *perspective* that a *narrative* takes toward the events it describes.

PROTAGONIST

The main *character* around whom the story revolves.

SETTING

The location of a *narrative* in time and space. Setting creates mood or atmosphere.

SUBPLOT

A secondary *plot* that is of less importance to the overall story but that may serve as a point of contrast or comparison to the main plot.

SYMBOL

An object, *character*, figure, or color that is used to represent an abstract idea or concept.

SYNTAX

The way the words in a piece of writing are put together to form lines, phrases, or clauses; the basic structure of a piece of writing.

THEME

A fundamental and universal idea explored in a literary work.

TONE

The author's attitude toward the subject or *characters* of a story or poem or toward the reader.

VOICE

An author's individual way of using language to reflect his or her own personality and attitudes. An author communicates voice through *tone*, *diction*, and *syntax*.

A Note on Plagiarism

Plagiarism—presenting someone else's work as your own—rears its ugly head in many forms. Many students know that copying text without citing it is unacceptable. But some don't realize that even if you're not quoting directly, but instead are paraphrasing or summarizing, it is plagiarism unless you cite the source.

Here are the most common forms of plagiarism:

- Using an author's phrases, sentences, or paragraphs without citing the source
- Paraphrasing an author's ideas without citing the source
- Passing off another student's work as your own

How do you steer clear of plagiarism? You should always acknowledge all words and ideas that aren't your own by using quotation marks around verbatim text or citations like footnotes and endnotes to note another writer's ideas. For more information on how to give credit when credit is due, ask your teacher for guidance or visit www.sparknotes.com.

REVIEW & RESOURCES

QUIZ

1. What kind of toy does Tabitha give Agnes to play with?

    A. A dollhouse
    B. A stuffed animal
    C. A puzzle
    D. A gyroscope

2. What story does Aunt Vidala tell in school that deeply upsets Becka?

    A. The story of Becka's mother
    B. The story of Genesis
    C. The story of a concubine
    D. The story of Baby Nicole

3. What does Neil keep in the safe in his office?

    A. A gun
    B. A microdot camera
    C. A backpack
    D. A mysterious toy

4. What profession did Aunt Lydia belong to, prior to the founding of Gilead?

    A. Politics
    B. Medicine
    C. Fashion
    D. Law

5. How did Aunt Adrianna, the Pearl Girl in Toronto, die?

    A. Her companion Pearl Girl killed her
    B. Suicide
    C. Mayday operatives murdered her
    D. Natural causes

6.   In what book does Aunt Lydia hide her manuscript?

    A.   *Inferno*, by Dante Alighieri
    B.   *Apologia Pro Vita Sua*, by Cardinal Newman
    C.   *Alice's Adventures in Wonderland*, by Lewis Carroll
    D.   *Persuasion*, by Jane Austen

7.   Why does Daisy cry the first time she speaks with the Pearl Girls in Toronto?

    A.   She's in pain
    B.   She suddenly feels overwhelmed with anger
    C.   She's afraid
    D.   She feels touched by their kindness

8.   What secret does Aunt Lydia have about Commander Judd?

    A.   He's a drug addict
    B.   He kills his wives
    C.   He has no money left
    D.   He's planning a high-profile assassination

9.   What symbol does Agnes embroider on the footstool square she makes prior to her betrothal to Commander Judd?

    A.   A string of pearls
    B.   A baby
    C.   A skull
    D.   A Handmaid's veil

10.   Which of the four founding Aunts helped plan the coup that toppled the United States government?

    A.   Aunt Elizabeth
    B.   Aunt Helena
    C.   Aunt Lydia
    D.   Aunt Vidala

11. What does Agnes learn about Paula from the top-secret folder she receives from an anonymous informant?

     A.   She murdered her first husband
     B.   She tried to have Agnes killed
     C.   She had an abortion
     D.   She helped her Handmaid escape to Canada

12. What does Becka use to try to commit suicide?

     A.   A knife
     B.   A gun
     C.   Pruning shears
     D.   A rope

13. When Aunt Lydia installed a hidden camera in her statue, who did she discover placing offerings there in an effort to incriminate Aunt Elizabeth?

     A.   Paula
     B.   Aunt Helena
     C.   Aunt Vidala
     D.   Commander Judd

14. Where did the militia men take Aunt Lydia after arresting her immediately after the coup?

     A.   A stadium
     B.   A big-box store
     C.   A high school
     D.   A parking lot

15. What was the real name of the Handmaid who died giving birth to Commander Kyle's child?

     A.   Jade
     B.   Nicole
     C.   Crystal
     D.   Victoria

16.   What revelation about Dr. Grove inspired Aunt Lydia to
      frame him for attempted rape?

      A.   He poisoned his wife
      B.   He molested Agnes
      C.   He molested Becka
      D.   He had ties to the Mayday resistance movement

17.   What kind of painting does Commander Judd have
      in his office?

      A.   A still-life
      B.   A pastoral with a female nude
      C.   A landscape
      D.   A portrait of a famous actress

18.   Who does Professor Pieixoto suggest may have been Agnes
      and Daisy's mother?

      A.   The author of the "Handmaid's Tale" tapes
      B.   Aunt Lydia
      C.   Ada
      D.   Commander Judd's first wife

19.   What causes Daisy to fall ill during her and Agnes's escape
      from Gilead?

      A.   Food poisoning
      B.   An infection
      C.   A virus
      D.   Sea sickness

20.   Who helps Agnes safely escape Paula's house to Ardua Hall?

      A.   Aunt Vidala
      B.   Aunt Estée
      C.   Her Marthas
      D.   Shunammite

21. According to Agnes, what is the source of the Aunts' power?

    A. Their ability to read
    B. Their collection of other peoples' secrets
    C. Their access to the Bloodlines Genealogical Record
    D. Their refusal of marriage

22. What did Aunt Lydia have to do to pass Commander Judd's test and become one of the four founding Aunts?

    A. Reveal the whereabouts of her loved ones
    B. Persuade other women to convert
    C. Participate in an execution of other women
    D. Provide sexual favors

23. Which of the following is *not* located in Gilead?

    A. SanctuCare
    B. Schlafly Café
    C. Margery Kempe Retreat Center
    D. Calm and Balm Clinic

24. Where in Ardua Hall does Becka hide to give Agnes and Daisy a head start on their escape?

    A. hidden compartment in her dormitory room
    B. The campus's outer wall
    C. A remote wing of the Hildegard library
    D. A rooftop water cistern

25. How does Aunt Lydia kill Aunt Vidala?

    A. She unplugs her life-support equipment
    B. She administers a lethal dose of morphine
    C. She adds poison to her IV drip
    D. She coerces Aunt Elizabeth to suffocate her

ANSWER KEY

1. A; 2. C; 3. B; 4. D; 5. A; 6. B; 7. D; 8. B; 9. C; 10. D; 11. A; 12. C; 13. C; 14. A; 15. C; 16. C; 17. B; 18. A; 19. B; 20. B; 21. B; 22. C; 23. A; 24. D; 25. D

Suggestions for Further Reading

Atwood, Margaret. *In Other Worlds: SF and the Human Imagination*. New York: Anchor Books, 2012.

Bouson, J. Brooks, ed. *Margaret Atwood: Critical Insights*. Ipswich, MA: Salem Press, 2013.

Curtis, Claire. *Postapocalyptic Fiction and the Social Contract: "We'll Not Go Home Again."* Lanham, MD: Lexington Books, 2010.

Kuźnicki, Sławomir. *Margaret Atwood's Dystopian Fiction: Fire Is Being Eaten*. Newcastle-Upon-Tyne, England: Cambridge Scholars Publishing, 2017.

Macpherson, Heidi Slettedahl. *The Cambridge Introduction to Margaret Atwood*. Cambridge: Cambridge University Press, 2010.

Sheckels, Theodore F. *The Political in Margaret Atwood's Fiction: The Writing on the Wall of the Tent*. London: Routledge, 2016.

Tolan, Fiona. *Margaret Atwood: Feminism and Fiction*. New York: Rodopi, 2007.

Waltonen, Karma, ed. *Margaret Atwood's Apocalypses*. Newcastle-Upon-Tyne, England: Cambridge Scholars Publishing, 2015.

Wisker, Gina. *Margaret Atwood: An Introduction to Critical Views of Her Fiction*. Houndmills, Basingstoke: Palgrave Macmillan, 2012.

NOTES

NOTES

NOTES

NOTES

NOTES